W9-CEU-711

0 00 30 0329126 1

4-10-03

HAYNER PUBLIC LIBRARY DISTRICT
ALTON, ILLINOIS

OVERDUES .10 PER DAY MAXIMUM FINE
COST OF BOOKS. LOST OR DAMAGED
BOOKS ADDITIONAL $5.00 SERVICE CHARGE.

# A Thin Difference

a novel by Frank Turner Hollon

MacAdam/Cage Publishing
155 Sansome Street, Suite 550
San Francisco, CA 94104
www.macadamcage.com
Copyright © 2003 by Frank Turner Hollon
ALL RIGHTS RESERVED.

Library of Congress Cataloging-in-Publication Data

Hollon, Frank Turner, 1963–
     A thin difference / by Frank Turner Hollon.
          p. cm.
     ISBN 1-931561-27-3 (Hardcover : alk. paper)
     1. Attorney and client–Fiction.  I. Title.

PS3608.O494 T48 2003
813'.54--dc21

                                        2002153578

Manufactured in the United States of America.
10 9 8 7 6 5 4 3 2 1

Book and jacket design by Dorothy Carico Smith

Publisher's Note: This is a work of fiction. Names, characters,
places, and incidents either are the product of the author's
imagination or are used fictitiously. Any resemblance to actual
events, locales, or persons, living or dead, is entirely coincidental.

F
HOL

AEJ-3177

A Thin Difference

a novel by Frank Turner Hollon

MacAdam/Cage

HAYNER PUBLIC LIBRARY DISTRICT
ALTON, ILLINOIS

*For my mother and father*

## CHAPTER 1

They never call before they rob the bank. It's always afterwards. After they've killed their wives, or sold a pound of dope at the truck stop, or raped the schoolgirl down the street. Then they call their lawyer. Then they want things to be like they used to be. Some men were never meant to be free. For some men, freedom burns like a meteorite flying through the atmosphere. They'd rather be dead than stay on fire.

I practiced law in south Alabama for thirty years. Mostly criminal defense. Everything else seemed cheap and secondhand. It's like the difference between the guy who fought World War I knee-deep in the trenches and the guy who drops bombs from the sky and never hears the explosions below that blow the guts out of men with photographs of their children in their back pockets. But I'm just the lawyer. I don't take the bullet or feel the concussion from the bomb. Usually, the lawyer goes home afterwards. Sometimes, the client doesn't.

I hear men say they love the law. I never loved the law. I loved the fight. The courtroom always felt like home. Maybe that's one of the reasons my marriages fell apart and my children ended up hating every bone in my body. I never felt at home with them like I did in front of a judge, or a jury, fighting the good fight, like a dog waiting for the moment when the flesh of the neck is exposed, and the teeth bury, and I can see the fear and acknowledgment in the eye of the wounded. That's the place to be, even if it's my neck exposed, and my eye with the flash of fear. Give me the goddamn fight, and stop whining.

My secretary was Rose. She was with me the entire thirty years. We sat one room apart, day after day, in the same office for thirty years, and I swear I couldn't tell you the names of her children. I slept in that office more nights than I care to remember. Rose always knew, but never said a word. She never said a word about the bottle of whiskey in my bottom drawer, or the female clients who on occasion exchanged services for services, or the cash that sometimes found its way into my pocket under Uncle Sam's table. To this day Rose Minnefield probably knows more about me than does any other human being on this earth. Unfortunately, most of the things she knows aren't good. I think she stuck with me all those years because she knew, no matter what, I fought for my clients. I fought just as hard for the poor ones as the rich ones, and just as hard for the guilty as the innocent. I always figured the American justice system functions only as well as its parts. If everybody does their job, the judge, the cops, the prosecutor, the defense attorney, and the jurors, justice tends to prevail. I can't help it if the other sons-of-bitches don't do their jobs.

My first wife took the children. The second wife

took the money. And the third wife, well, when she left she took with her my fondness for women in general. I have to laugh when I think about her, standing in the kitchen, arms crossed, explaining how she fell in love with the plumber. His name was Jake. I imagine Jake has had the opportunity by now to see her standing in another kitchen, arms crossed, explaining about the new handyman.

I can't blame her though. She got out while the gettin' was good. The first two wives waited far too long. They had more of me than any woman deserves. And now they both have good husbands who raised my children. Men, I'm sure, who have learned to resent me for placing them in the dreaded stepfather role. They provided stability for my children, food, medical insurance. They coached Little League baseball, went to swim meets, stayed up all night on Christmas Eve, and yet, hidden deep in the minds of the children was the knowledge that these men, despite their sacrifices, were not and never would be their father. The feeling cannot be placed in words but exists as a colorless and tasteless poison in every glance and awkward hug.

What they don't know is my position in the hate game. If I work too hard, I'm a cold workaholic. If I don't provide financially, I'm a deadbeat dad. Besides, I'm the one who ruined their lives. I'm the guy who had the power to make their lives divine and chose instead to satisfy my selfish urges, one by one, until the house of cards and the white picket fence blew away in the winds of decadence.

My financial problems started when Wanda (wife

number two) hired a private investigator who followed me to all my nasty haunting grounds. She got the house, alimony, and most everything else. I was already neck-deep in child support and back taxes. The hole got deeper and deeper. Once again, the only refuge was the courtroom. The purity of the confrontation. I just kept working and working, blinded and frustrated. It was this blindness and frustration that dulled my instincts. Instincts I spent my life sharpening and trusting. Generally, I can sit across my desk from a person and know everything I need to know about them in five minutes. But on one occasion, one important occasion, I let my guard down. I let the need for money cloud my judgment. The desire for the fight kept my eyes straight ahead, and the man who keeps his eyes straight ahead has a hard time watching his back.

CHAPTER 2

I met Brad Caine on a Monday. He was sitting quietly in my lobby with a briefcase next to his chair when I came around the corner from my office. My tie was loose at the top and my shirt-sleeves were rolled up.

"What can I do ya for?" I asked.

"You Jack Skinner?"

"You the tax man?"

"No," Brad Caine said.

"Then I'm Jack Skinner."

He stood and we shook hands. A firm shake, not too hard, not limp, and not too long. One solid up and down and a clean release. He was early thirties, short hair, with a jacket, no tie. He was clean-shaven, about six feet tall, not fat, not skinny.

"I'm Brad Caine. I was gonna make an appointment, but nobody was here."

I shuffled through a stack of files on Rose's desk and said, "Yeah, Rose goes to lunch every day around noon. I haven't been able to break the woman of her eating habit."

Brad Caine laughed slightly.

"How long you been here?" I asked.

"Only a few minutes. Since about twelve-fifteen."

I looked at the clock on the wall. I don't wear a watch, never have.

"My morning case got continued. I've got time right now if you wanna sit down. No sense makin' an appointment I probably won't be able to keep anyway. I stay in court most of the time, and I'm scheduled to be back up there this afternoon."

"That'll be fine," Brad Caine said.

He followed me down the hall to my office. Whenever I walked down that hallway I always wondered what it smelled like to outsiders. I knew damn well I couldn't smell anymore the sour odor of the carpet in the kitchen with twenty-year-old coffee stains. Sometimes, on warm days, I could still smell the tobacco smoke sealed in the walls and ceiling from before I quit. Not a day passed without the desire to light up a Marlboro Red and rest my feet up top the old mahogany desk.

"Have a seat, young man," I pointed, and then sat down behind my desk. "What's your story?"

I pulled a half-used yellow legal pad from a stack near the phone and put pen to paper. I asked the same first question I ask every client.

"What's your mailing address?"

"Well, I don't have one down here yet. I'm moving from Birmingham. That's what I'm here to see you about."

Mr. Caine smiled. "I need your help. I plan to open a sports bar down here. I've been working in sales the last few years up in Birmingham, saving my money. Gulf Shores doesn't have a good sports bar. Every beach town should have a place where people can drink beer and watch a game together."

I watched him as he spoke. Like I said earlier, I can usually learn more from a person in the first five minutes than I learn the rest of their lives. Brad Caine seemed fairly well educated, but didn't grow up a rich boy. He was a salesman, but he wasn't afraid to stare me straight in the eye, and I'm a pretty difficult bastard to stare in the eye.

"And what exactly do you need me for?" I asked.

"Well, I need a liquor license, and I've got a small problem. I've got a few felony convictions from when I was younger. I'm sure you know a man can't get a liquor license with a felony conviction. I need to hire you to get my record expunged and help me get the license. I may not be a rocket scientist, but I'm smart enough to know I'm gonna need a local guy to get things done down here."

Lawyers' fees fluctuate based upon the potential client's ability to pay. If you quote too high, you can scare them away. If you quote too low, you kick yourself later. An old lawyer once told me, "If the guy's head doesn't fly back when you quote your fee, you went too low."

"Before I take a client, Mr. Caine, I like to know exactly what I'm being hired to do. Besides expunging your criminal record and helping you to get a liquor license for your sports bar in Gulf Shores, what else would I be helping you with?"

"I'll need to get my business started, become a corporation, maybe keep you on retainer to help with my legal problems."

Brad Caine looked at me for a moment before he said, "You're a man who gets things done. I didn't just walk in here off the street. A guy in Birmingham referred you to me."

"Who?" I asked.

"Charlie Allen."

The name didn't ring a bell, but that was nothing unusual. I had a habit of asking each new client how they got to me and half the time I didn't recognize the name of the person who sent them in my direction. In thirty years of practicing law I had represented thousands of people, not to mention the witnesses and cops and jurors I came into contact with each working day.

"What kind of felony convictions do you have, and where?"

"Burglaries. In Birmingham. Jefferson County."

A nice round number was forming in my mind for the fee. Before I opened my mouth, Brad Caine reached into his inside coat pocket and pulled out a brown envelope.

"Like I said, I've been saving my money. I'm not married, I don't have any kids. Every penny has been set aside, and I know almost exactly how much I'll need."

He leaned over to hand me the envelope.

He spoke again, "I set aside five thousand dollars for the legal expenses. It's in cash. Will that be a problem?"

In the old days I would have leaned back in my big chair and surveyed the situation. But like an old bear, I'd gotten lazy, and of course, like a hungry bear, I needed the fuckin' money. I took the envelope.

"What will our arrangement be?" he asked.

"I'll put this in my trust account and work on an hourly basis. You'll get a bill from me at the end of each month broken down into tenths of hours. You'll be able to tell how I'm spending my time for you. I'll pay myself out of your retainer each month until it's gone. After that, we start all over."

"What do you need from me?" Brad Caine asked.

"A mailing address, your business paperwork, and whatever else you want me to have in my file," I said. "And by the way, don't call here five times a day. I'll call you back when I get out of court. Don't drive Rose crazy."

I looked at the clock on the wall. It was twelve forty-five. I hadn't had lunch yet, and I was due in court by two o'clock.

I opened the envelope and counted the money out loud. It was all there. I put it back in the brown envelope and dropped it in the middle right-hand drawer of my desk.

"You hungry?" I asked.

"I haven't eaten lunch yet."

"Let's walk across the street to the diner. It ain't bad. Sometimes Linda slips me a free piece of pie."

We stood to leave, and I walked around my desk. Brad Caine asked, "Is it O.K. for me to leave my briefcase here? I'll grab it after lunch."

"Sure," I said, and then asked, "Have you got a place down here yet?"

He slid the black case between the trash can and the

bookcase around the far side of the desk. We walked past Rose's empty chair and continued our conversation out the door.

"No. I'll have to call or come back by in the next few days and give your secretary my address and phone number and the other information you'll need. I don't want to pull the trigger on any deal until I find out about the liquor license. How hard is it to expunge a record?"

"It depends. It depends on the record, and the judge, and a few other things. I've been doin' this a long time. There's more than one way to skin a cat."

We sat down in my favorite booth in the corner. I couldn't figure out whether I liked the guy or not. It didn't really matter. In my financial state, for the right money, I probably would have bent over the booth if he asked me to. Five thousand dollars was the right money. But he didn't know that.

We both ordered the special. Meatloaf, mashed potatoes, and green beans. The clock on the wall said 1:15.

Somewhere in the middle of the conversation Brad Caine asked, "You wouldn't happen to know anyone in the market for a nice gold and diamond necklace?"

He pulled it out of the same inside jacket pocket where he'd gotten the brown envelope. There were clear diamond-like stones embedded in the gold.

"Where'd you get it?" I asked.

"A guy down here owed me money. He offered to pay his debt with his wife's necklace. I got tired of arguing with the guy and just took it."

"You better hope it ain't stolen."

I took a big bite of meatloaf and talked while I chewed.

"There was a time I would've taken it off your hands and given it to a woman. I've pissed away my share of money through the years on jewelry for women. Not anymore."

At one-thirty we walked out of the diner. I had thirty minutes to grab my file and get to the courthouse for a hearing in front of Judge Stone.

Brad Caine stopped at the small red car and pulled his keys from his pocket. He held out his hand and we shook.

"It was nice to meet you, Mr. Skinner. I'll be in touch tomorrow or the next day. I hope you can help me."

"I hope so, too," I said, and then we parted.

Rose was back from lunch. I retrieved the brown envelope and dropped it on her desk.

"While you were out eating caviar and drinking martinis, I hooked a nice size fish."

Rose opened the envelope.

"Did you give the fish a receipt?"

"No."

Rose frowned. "Are you ever gonna learn?"

"Probably not, Rose. Probably not."

I put on my jacket in a hurry, scooped up my file, and headed for the door. Next to the trash can on the far side of my desk I saw the corner of Brad Caine's black briefcase. He had forgotten to come back and get it. The phone rang. Rose told the caller I had already left to court. I tiptoed past her and got away.

CHAPTER 3

That night, when I got back from court, I stayed in the office until after eight o'clock. It's amazing how much work I used to get done simply because I had nowhere else to go. That first cool glass of whiskey almost always would set my mind in a new direction sitting behind my desk.

I can't remember the last time I had sex. I can't even remember the last time I really wanted to. Don't get me wrong, lust still survived, but it existed in a separate place. Somewhere down the line I must have decided it just wasn't worth the effort. Desire was no longer a command, just a low whisper.

My car had more than two hundred thousand miles on it. I got it as a fee from a guy charged with diddling half the boys in his neighborhood. I often wondered if he had done any of his diddling in that old white car. I had long since stopped worrying about whether clients were impressed with my vehicle. Anyone impressed by a car isn't worth impressing in the first place. It's nothing but a big lawnmower with a radio.

On the way home I stopped at Buddy's Bar & Grill

and asked Lola to fix me a cheeseburger to go. Lola's cheeseburgers were big and fat and greasy the way God intended cheeseburgers to be. I drove home in the old white car with the cheeseburger resting comfortably in a white bag on the passenger seat where my dirty client probably reached over with his dirty hand to rub a ten-year-old boy scared out of his wits.

I had an apartment less than a mile from my office. It was dark and depressing, and I liked it that way. Men were born to live in caves, and my cave was my castle. Nobody made me pick up my clothes or throw away old newspapers. I yanked off my tie, settled down on the couch, took a bite of my cheeseburger and pulled the fresh newspaper from its thin plastic wrapper. I didn't care much for television, never have. Those idiots just babble endlessly. If one of those T.V. news anchor people knocked on my door and asked to come inside to personally report the news to me, I'd slam the door shut and hope the breeze ruffled their perfect hair. I prefer the newspaper. It's quiet.

On page one of the paper was an article about an old lady found dead in her beach house in Gulf Shores. I recognized her name. Haddie Charles. She owed me money, over twenty thousand dollars in attorney's fees from a case I worked on for almost five years. It was a lawsuit against her sisters for stealing the family fortune. There's nothing like a family lawsuit to boil the blood. Rich people lose all sense of financial responsibility and pay their lawyers ungodly amounts of money, or in the case of Haddie Charles, promise to pay their lawyers ungodly amounts of money, well earned I might add. Maybe that's how the rich stay rich.

I put my cheeseburger down on the wrapper and leaned over the newspaper spread across the coffee table. Gulf Shores is a coastal city on the Gulf of Mexico about thirty miles from my office. In the old days it mostly consisted of beach houses and seafood restaurants. In the past twenty years the town had grown into a mecca for tourists and snowbirds. Haddie Charles was neither. She was a longtime local from a wealthy family.

The article said the old lady was found dead in her home where she lived alone. Investigator Randy Riley was quoted as saying, "She appears to have died from blunt force injuries to the head. We can't speculate at this time about possible suspects or a motive."

I can't read a newspaper article involving a crime without dissecting the situation and reading between the lines. Maybe her half-crippled older sister got tired of the bullshit and cracked her skull. I can't say I was sorry. I never much liked her. She carried herself like certain rich people who never have worked for a living and somehow decide they are better because of it. It always seemed the opposite to me. The most useless people I've ever known had a trust fund hanging under them like a safety net or an inheritance waiting just around the corner of their daddy's deathbed. What a horrible feeling. Never knowing the satisfaction of earning your own way. Always knowing, somewhere in the back of your mind, that someone else used their sweat, or their genius, to earn the money that pays for the food that makes you fat and the gin that slowly burns away your guilt.

I have rolled ungracefully too many times in courtroom victories against big city lawyers with their big city suits. They refuse to admit defeat and instead prefer to drown their losses in a sea of paperwork and appeals. But there is a moment, sometimes terribly brief, when the jury announces the verdict and the rich big city lawyer doesn't have time to disguise the shock. You should see it. Beautiful. Their clients look at them out of the corner of their eyes. What went wrong? Why can't you beat that washed-up old lawyer who needs to lose twenty pounds and drives a white car with two hundred thousand miles?

I finished reading about Haddie Charles and pictured her on the peach carpet of her beach house with a red ring of blood around her white hair.

There was an article on page two about lawyers. A survey listed attorneys as the third least trusted people in our society next to politicians and car salesmen. Where do they come up with that shit? Some of the most trustworthy people I've ever known in my life are lawyers. People want to believe lawyers are ruthless and unethical so they can utilize these talents when they get caught themselves doing whatever bad thing they do. It gives them hope.

I've got a cat named Echo, but I hate cats. When my third wife left with the plumber I refused to give her the cat. It was my only victory, but then, years later, I found myself stuck with a cat I never liked in the first place. And by the way, I sure as hell didn't name the cat Echo. Who would name a cat Echo? Why name a cat at all? The animal refused to acknowledge or appreciate my sacrifices, much less respond to its name. We stared at each other sometimes. Mostly when I ate.

"What are you lookin' at?" I said.

No response.

CHAPTER 4

Two days later, late Wednesday morning, Rose yelled out to me from the other room, "Collect call on line one from the jail. It's Brad Caine. That's the guy I just opened a file for. Why's he in jail?"

It was a good question. I was curious and told Rose to accept the call.

"Hello."

"Mr. Skinner?"

"Yes."

"I'm in jail."

"No shit. What happened?"

"Remember that necklace I showed you?"

"Yes."

"You were right. It was stolen. I got arrested trying to sell it."

"Is it just one charge of receiving stolen property?" I asked.

There was a moment of hesitation.

"It's a lot worse than that, Mr. Skinner. They say it belonged to some rich lady who was murdered in her house."

"Haddie Charles?"

"Yeah, that's the name. They said it was stolen a few days ago when she was killed. They think I killed the lady. I swear to God I didn't kill anyone. I got that necklace from a guy named Edward Polston. He owed me five hundred dollars, and I took the necklace for payment on his debt like I told you the other day."

"Have you talked to the cops?"

"I only told 'em what I just told you. Some investigator from Gulf Shores named Riley."

"Keep your mouth shut, Brad. Don't talk to anyone. Don't call anyone on the phone. Just sit still until I get there."

I hung up.

The only assistant district attorney I trusted was Deborah Webb. She was a good lawyer, a career prosecutor, knew her way around the courtroom, and was fair and square. I called her immediately.

"Deborah?"

"Yes."

"It's Jack Skinner."

"That mean old bastard down in Loxley?"

"Yes, that's the one. What can you tell me about Brad Caine?"

"Is he yours?"

"I'm afraid so," I said. I smelled a weakness.

"Well, we just drafted the warrant for capital murder. He was arrested first on the receiving charge. It's too early to tell you much."

"Just give me an idea, Deborah. I'm gonna find out sooner or later."

"Did you read about the lady in Gulf Shores murdered in her home?"

"I saw it, but I didn't pay much attention to it."

"Your boy sold her stolen jewelry. We can put his car in the neighborhood on the afternoon before she was killed, Sunday. How much do you know about your boy?"

"Not much."

I could hear Deborah shuffling through papers. She said, "He's got a sheet that stretches halfway across my desk. Burglary arrests and convictions mostly."

"How long ago?" I asked.

"The last one was six years ago in Birmingham."

"He's a changed man, Deborah."

"I've heard that before."

"Did he give a statement?"

"He told Riley he got the necklace from a guy named Edward Polston, but we can't find anybody by that name. He says he didn't get down here until Monday morning when he met with you, but we've got witnesses putting his car in her neighborhood. I'm not telling you any more right now."

We hung up cordially. It was weak. It sounded like they decided Brad Caine was guilty and didn't want his ass out of jail because he might disappear. It sounded like they had a lot of work to do in the investigation.

I drove thirty miles to the Baldwin County Jail and ended up in the conference room waiting for the guard to get Brad Caine. Brad was dressed in the standard orange jumpsuit with his hands cuffed in the front. We sat down and looked at each other through the heavy wire screen.

"I've done some stupid shit in my life, Mr. Skinner, but I never killed anybody, and I didn't steal that lady's jewelry."

"Where'd you get the necklace?"

"Before I came to your office I met this guy, Edward Polston, to get my money. He said it belonged to his wife."

"Where can I find him?"

"I met him at McDonald's parking lot in Loxley. He's probably a million miles from here by now."

He seemed scared, but not out of his mind.

"Can you get me outta here?"

"No. There's no bond for capital murder. You'll sit here until you go to trial, or they drop the charges. And don't expect the charges to be dropped. Even if they've gotten ahead of themselves. Unless they find the guy who really did this, I think you need to expect a trial."

Brad Caine lowered his head and rubbed his eyes.

"Will you represent me, Mr. Skinner?"

"Yeah, I will. But it might cost you more than five thousand dollars for a capital murder trial. If you're convicted, they'll send you to death row, guaranteed. The judges in this county give the death sentence whenever they get the chance, and if a jury says you killed this helpless old lady for her necklace, you can count on a death sentence."

He was listening to what I said, but his eyes drifted over my head to a spot on the wall.

Brad Caine whispered, "I didn't do it."

I believed him. A criminal lawyer's heaviest burden is an innocent client. There is no pressure like the

knowledge that the man next to you at the table is innocent and will die if the job isn't done right. One wrong
question, one moment when the mind drifts from the
course. But God help me, I loved it.

"Do you have anybody you want me to call, mother
or father?"

Brad's eyes snapped back from the place on the wall
to my face.

"No," he said. "It's just me."

"Keep your mouth shut in here. The place is full of
snitches lookin' to use information to save their own
skin. And don't talk on the phone. They're not supposed
to tape-record your conversations with your lawyer, but I
don't trust most of these bastards. You talk only to me,
and only in person.

"I'll file some motions in the next few days and
request a preliminary hearing to learn as much as we can.
You're in jail and this is a capital charge so your case will
have priority. We can push it to trial in five or six
months if we need to."

I stood to leave. Brad Caine stood up across from me.

"Mr. Skinner, I don't mean to sound dramatic, but
you're all I've got. I can't help myself in here. I can't do
anything to prove I didn't do it."

Before I walked out the door I said, "Brad, you don't
have to prove you *didn't* do it. They have to prove you
*did*. There's a big difference."

I started to leave and then remembered. "You forgot
your briefcase at my office."

"Yeah, I know. They won't let me have it in here.
Can you just hold on to it until I figure out what to do?"

He had that look. The look I've seen before. Like he couldn't believe what was happening to him. Like it was a bad dream, and he couldn't wake up.

On the way home I stopped at the McDonald's in Loxley. On my notepad I jotted a diagram of the layout of the parking lot. At the drive-through window I got a Big Mac for dinner. My mind was flying in all directions, and I tried to write down the ideas as I drove.

Find Edward Polston

Make and model of B's car?

Tire tracks?

Fingerprints?

Anything else stolen from the house?

B's prior burglaries? Same method?

Who did B try to sell jewelry to?

Murder weapon?

Haddie Charles was killed Sunday evening. Sitting in my office Monday at lunchtime, did Brad Caine look or act like a man who just bludgeoned to death an old lady eighteen hours earlier? I've been fooled before, but not often. There were lots of questions to answer.

Back at my apartment I found the newspaper from Monday and cut out the article for my file. Haddie Charles was seventy-eight years old. I looked up from my paper to see Echo watching me from the chair as I started to unwrap the Big Mac. I pinched a piece of burger from the edge and tossed it toward the cat. The meat bounced off the cushion of the chair and rolled in front of the television. The cat didn't move a muscle.

CHAPTER 5

Becky, my oldest daughter, decided she was the spokesman for my children. I'm not sure if she's a bitch all the time, or only when she talks to me. She uses any means necessary. It must be an interesting way to live, having a built-in excuse for every failure. Apparently, I'm personally and directly responsible for Becky's failed marriage (her husband got caught with a prostitute face-down in his lap at the park), Mark's inability to keep a job (he likes to sleep late), and Kelly's drug habit. It's hard to give a shit about any of them, and it's even harder not to.

"Father?" Becky said on the other end of the phone.

"Yes, Becky."

"I need to meet with you."

Sarcastically I said, "Let's have lunch together. You can tell me how happy you are."

"Don't be an asshole."

"I'm trying not to be an asshole. I'd just like, one time, for you to call and say something good. Anything. A conversation that doesn't include moral negotiations, or calling me an asshole, or dragging up something I said twenty years ago."

My words never fazed Becky. She was entrenched in her position, solid in her mission, unaffected by reason or emotion. And her ass was large.

"It's about Kelly."

Kelly was my weakness. My baby girl. The youngest, the most fragile, the most screwed up. Even at twenty-eight years old, she simply was incapable of existing in this world on a day-to-day basis, and despite Becky, I always felt responsible. I knew I wasn't the cause of Mark's lazy godless disposition, I knew I wasn't responsible for Becky's constant bitter aftertaste or the failure of her marriage, but when it came to Kelly, the sight of her in desperation left me sick. And Becky knew it.

"I'll be over at the office before lunch," she said, and hung up the phone.

I once got a call in the middle of the night from a client. He told me my daughter was lying in the gutter behind a bar in downtown Pensacola. She was seventeen. I drove alone for forty-five minutes to Pensacola filling my head with what I imagined I would see when I got there. But in between the images, I saw my baby daughter, as a little girl, in her yellow Easter dress, cupping her hands around her mouth telling me she loved me. I cried. Jesus, I cried so hard I couldn't see the highway. It was uncontrollable, and I had to pull over on the side of the road. I never told anybody about it. No one. Who could I have told?

I found her right where he said she would be, on a back street in the dark. Two guys were sitting next to her on the curb. Kelly was mumbling with her face cheek-down against the pavement, her long brown hair wet. Kelly's blue jeans were unbuttoned and down a few inches from her waist.

I pulled the pistol from underneath my coat and held it to the head of the closest man sitting next to Kelly. He froze like a statue, and kept his eyes straight ahead.

"Did you touch her?" I said calmly.

"No, sir. This is how we found her. I swear it."

The other guy looked up at me through a haze of drugs and alcohol. If he could have seen himself, he'd have begged me to blow his head off.

I lifted my daughter from the gutter and held her in my arms. She wedged her face into the warmth of my neck, and I walked her back to the car. Before that night, I knew something was wrong with her, but I had no idea of the depth. It was an endless hole, black and dark, like a well deep in the earth. I could drop a rock and never hear it hit the bottom. If you do not have a child, you can never understand.

Just before noon, Becky walked past Rose and straight into my office. She sat down. At thirty-two years old she looked fifty-two. Sometimes it was hard to remember if she was my daughter or some long-lost ex-wife.

"Are you really representing that man who killed Haddie Charles? I knew her."

"Well, Becky, I'm representing the man they've accused of killing Haddie Charles."

"Never mind," she said. "I don't have time for your word games."

Her face was stone. She was the self-appointed

hardass.

"Kelly's using again. She's at the shelter on the Causeway. I need seven hundred dollars to get her back in the drug program."

I already had the checkbook on the desk. I wrote while she spoke.

The door was open, and I knew Rose was listening. She hated Becky. I wrote out, "Seven hundred dollars and no cents."

"They say he got caught selling Haddie's jewelry."

I slid the check across the desk. More than the other children, Becky looked like me. The day she was born the nurse looked at the baby, looked at me, and said, "You don't have to wonder where this one came from." Maybe that's the reason we couldn't have a decent conversation. It was like talking to myself in the mirror.

I waited for Becky to leave before I got in my car and drove to the shelter on the Causeway. Kelly was asleep on a cot. She was always so beautiful, like her mother. Soft and breakable, not for this world. She reminded me of what an angel would look like. I sat down on the cot next to her. On the other side was a drunk guy I recognized from night court. He spent his life crawling in and out of a bottle. I could smell him.

"Hey, Daddy," Kelly whispered. She smiled like she was a little girl and I was waking her on Christmas morning.

"Hey, baby girl."

There were dark circles under Kelly's eyes and a small cut above her left eyebrow. She was wearing a T-shirt I'd never seen before. Her little bare feet stuck out from the edge of the blanket. I reached my hand over and touched her hair.

"Why do you do this to yourself, Kelly?"

The smile faded away. "I don't know."

"I gave your sister some money. She'll probably be down here soon to get you back in rehab."

"I know," she said.

There was a television in the corner of the room. The noon news announced the arrest of Brad Caine, and I heard my name spoken as his attorney. Kelly's eyes watched as they flashed the mug shot of Brad and told of the murder of Haddie Charles.

Kelly said, "I can tell by his face. He didn't kill her."

"You never know," I answered. "Sometimes their faces lie, but I think we've got a chance."

Kelly smiled again. "If you're his lawyer, he's got a chance."

"You think so?"

"Yes, I think so. Didn't you tell me once that old Haddie Charles owed you money and she wouldn't sell any of her family jewelry to pay you what she owed?"

"That's true. I don't suppose I'll get it now, will I?"

We were quiet for several minutes.

"Daddy, do you remember the time, when I was a little girl, you took me to my first day of school?"

I pictured her little face in my mind. We drove together from the house to school. Kelly wore a blue dress and held her lunch box in her lap. She stared straight ahead at the dashboard of the car, and I felt like I was taking her to a place where I would never see her again.

I stopped the car in front of the school. Kelly turned

to me with tears down her cheeks and said, "Don't worry, Daddy. I'll be O.K."

She wasn't O.K. She would never be. I looked down at her on the cot, asleep again, and then walked away from the shelter. Every time I saw her, I knew it could be the last. Every time was like the day I took her to school.

A week before the preliminary hearing was scheduled I met with Deborah Webb in the district attorney's office to learn what I could.

"Stop scaring all the secretaries."

"What secretaries?" I asked.

Deborah laughed. "All the women in the office are afraid of you. You stomp around like a grumpy grizzly bear."

She was probably right. I didn't even notice anymore. It was part of the lawyer intimidation game.

"Tell me about the Haddie Charles case."

"Can't you wait until the preliminary hearing?" she said.

"I'm here to take advantage of the 'open file' policy of the Baldwin County District Attorney's office on capital murder cases."

"Now Jack, we both know the 'open file' policy doesn't officially take effect until a discovery order is entered. We don't even have an indictment yet."

It was the dance of discovery. Almost like the flirtation of a first date. Later, there would be days we hated each other, and we both knew this case had the potential to bring out the best and worst of each of us.

"Tell me what you can."

Deborah pulled several folders from a file.

"The right-hand side of her skull was crushed. Your boy is left-handed. There's a load of jewelry missing, and maybe some other things. We've got the family members making lists of what they remember in the house, but she apparently wasn't very close to her family anymore. Total missing jewelry is worth over a million dollars.

"Mr. Caine is on videotape trying to sell a necklace. Unfortunately for him, he approached a guy who got indicted by the Feds a few months ago, and the guy decided he could help himself by reporting the call he got from Mr. Caine. The FBI set up a buy, put a wire on the guy, and videotaped the whole thing in a motel room. You'll see it all at the hearing. Your boy says a few interesting things." Deborah grinned. "Is that enough?"

"Don't stop now. You're on a roll."

"The house was entered through the attic. The alarm wasn't set. Mr. Caine has several prior burglaries. He entered the house through the attic."

I kept notes as she spoke.

"Two separate witnesses identified your boy's car in the neighborhood Sunday afternoon. One even got a partial tag number. Mr. Caine lied to us about when he got down here from Birmingham. We can't find this person named Edward Polston he says gave him the jewelry. There was an Edward Polston arrested for DUI a year ago, but we haven't been able to find him."

On the surface it sounded bad, but both of us knew

it was all circumstantial except for the sale of the jewelry. If Edward Polston showed up and verified Brad's story, the case could fall apart quickly.

"Oh, yeah," Deborah said, "the old lady's ring finger was cut off with a hacksaw. At least we think it was a hacksaw. The autopsy report is weeks away."

"Did you find the ring?" I asked.

"No."

"Did you find a murder weapon?"

"No, but there's a missing brass bookend."

"Was it a one-man job?"

"Maybe, maybe not," she said.

"You got any fingerprints?"

"You'll have to wait for that."

"Do you have any tire tracks?"

"Nope. All cement."

"When can I get the police reports?"

"You'll get most of them at the hearing. After the indictment, you can have everything I've got."

I reviewed my notes. Deborah organized her file and said, "He did it, Jack. It's just a matter of us building the case piece by piece."

"Really? This is what I heard while I've been sitting here. You've got no fingerprints, no DNA, no prior connection between Brad Caine and Haddie Charles. You've got no confession, no witness to put him at the scene, no murder weapon, no finger, and no idea whatsoever where Edward Polston is hiding while he tries to sell the rest of the jewelry he stole from Haddie Charles when he killed her."

I pushed myself up from the leather chair.

I added, "When I came here I had my doubts about Brad Caine. You just convinced me he's an innocent man. If this is as good as it gets, good luck."

Deborah smiled. "Have a good day, Grizzly Bear."

CHAPTER 7

On the night before the preliminary hearing I scheduled a meeting at Buddy's Bar & Grill with a private
investigator named Junior Miflin. I got there early and
sat at the bar alone. My wallet was fat. I had decided earlier that day to transfer Brad's five thousand dollars from
the trust account to my general account and consider it
a fee. It wouldn't last long. I was three months behind on
rent, the malpractice insurance premium was due, I
owed the accountant, the cleaning service, Rose, and
the kid who fixed the fax machine. Rose and the kid
were last in line. The tax man had a lien on everything
I owned, but I'll be damned if he could stop me from
having a cheeseburger and a cool glass of whiskey.

There was a jukebox at Buddy's. The place always
smelled like a cigarette was burning in the ashtray next to
your elbow. It was a refuge for the lonely. People shot pool
and got drunk and lit each other's cigarettes. They flirted
with other men's ugly wives with the subtlety of a bull-
dozer. I had represented most of the people in the room
through the years and they called me "Lawyer Jack."

Junior Miflin showed up. He had the face of a

squirrel and chewed his fingernails incessantly. He was always nervous.

"Why do you come to this place?" Junior asked.

"They've got good cheeseburgers. You want one?"

"No."

I pulled an envelope of cash from my inside coat pocket and handed it to Junior.

"This is a down payment from Brad Caine, the guy they arrested for killing Haddie Charles."

Junior's stubby fingers opened the envelope and counted the bills.

"I need you to find a guy named Edward Polston. He got a DUI in the county about a year ago. He won't be easy to find. By now he knows everybody's looking for him. We need to find him before the cops. He's the key to this damn thing."

Junior Miflin's eyes darted back and forth from the pool table to the front door.

Just for fun I said, "Why you so nervous, Junior?"

"I'm not nervous."

He folded the envelope and shoved it in the back pocket of his blue jeans. On a white bar napkin he wrote E-d-w-a-r-d P-o-l-s-t-o-n.

"What else?"

"See what you can find out about anybody lookin' to sell some high-quality jewelry."

I took a bite of my cheeseburger.

"What else?"

"My friend, Mr. Caine, has prior burglary arrests and convictions. See if you can find out if he works alone."

Junior jotted a few notes on the napkin. I swirled the

brown whiskey around the glass and took a big sip.

"When do you need it?" he asked.

"As soon as you can get it," I answered.

I watched Junior walk out the door. Through the years I've learned how completely a lawyer can lose perspective on a case. I have looked back and seen how buried I sometimes became. It's a mechanism of protection. The deeper I become, the more necessary it is to believe in something. Sometimes I would hang my hat on innocence, but more often it was something vague like the unfairness of the law, or the violation of rights, or the defendant's victimization by circumstance. It takes years to regain enough clarity looking back to truly balance whether justice was done. As I took another sip of whiskey sitting at Buddy's, I could feel myself on the edge of the slippery slope of the adversarial system. It was a fight worth fighting. The case wouldn't go away. The D.A.'s office had put itself in a corner with the early arrest, but I certainly understood their reasons. There were no co-defendants to turn, too much publicity, and a dead old lady on the floor of her home. With Brad Caine's prior convictions there would be no plea bargain, and my instincts told me Brad wouldn't accept one anyway.

As I finished the first drink, my daughter Kelly walked into the bar.

"Hey, Daddy."

"What are you doing here, Kelly? Why aren't you where you're supposed to be?"

She smiled, "Daddy, wherever you are is where you're supposed to be."

"I don't think Buddy's Bar & Grill is where you're supposed to be."

She sat down on the stool next to me, and I saw again the scar above her eyebrow.

"Where'd you get that scar?"

"I don't remember. Let's go to a movie. I haven't been to a movie in years."

Whenever I found myself in Kelly's presence, we were surrounded by the color of guilt. I would remember very specific incidents. I came home from work one day. She was probably six or seven years old. Before I had time to make the change from lawyer mode to family mode, Kelly knocked the remote control off the arm of the couch and pieces bounced across the floor. I spanked her hard. Too hard. At first she didn't cry. At first she just looked at me with fear. Fear of her own father, and what I was capable of doing in a flash of anger.

We went to a movie that night after we left Buddy's. In the lobby I saw a man standing next to a video machine watching Kelly. I didn't recognize him, but I recognized the look of dangerous desperation, the unshaven face, the angry cut of his eyes. Kelly walked to him while I stood in the popcorn line. He touched her arm. His words were sharp. Drug addicts find each other in the underbelly of America. They are drawn together by addiction and the search to satisfy the unholy hunger. The man looked at me watching and took his hand from her arm. Kelly turned to see me and strolled away like nothing.

"Who was that man?" I asked.

"Nobody. Just a guy I know."

You would think I'd have learned not to care, but it isn't really an option. It isn't something to be learned.

"When you're with me, when we're together, don't talk to that man. I can't do anything about the people you choose when I'm not around, but when we're together, just walk past them and let me believe what I want to believe."

After the movie Kelly asked me to drop her off at a restaurant. She said she was meeting some friends. I knew there was a hole-in-the-wall bar around the corner from the restaurant, and I knew as soon as my car was out of sight she would slide in the door of that bar and sit next to a man like the one in the lobby of the theater, maybe even the same man. But I drove away anyway.

When I got home, Echo sat on the welcome mat at the door of the apartment. Next to her was a dead mole, small and gray and blind. She brought me gifts regularly. I'm told some cats bring gifts and some don't. Echo was a gift giver. Every few days she brought a bird, or a mouse, or a skink. Sometimes she would wait on the mat until I opened the door from the inside and then she would dart across the threshold with the prize hanging from her mouth. One night I chased a brown mouse around the apartment with a shoe until I finally gave up and agreed to allow the mouse to share my home. I never saw him again.

Echo was proud of the dead mole. She felt she had earned her room and board. I wondered if the landlord would accept the dead mole as a partial payment on the rent.

I had visited Brad Caine several times in jail, but sitting next to me in the courtroom he looked much more like the man who had come to my office that Monday morning. He carried himself with a gentle confidence, not cocky or arrogant, but like a man who believed his ordeal would be over soon and he could go about his life.

The preliminary hearing was nothing more than a formality, a chance for me to dig for details and try to corner Investigator Randy Riley in his testimony. It was also a chance for the press to come down like vultures on a fresh kill. They roamed the hallways like hyperactive school kids who missed their Ritalin. I tried to sow the seeds of doubt knowing almost everyone in our eventual jury pool would read or see something about the case of Haddie Charles. It was big news, and one of my jobs was to try to use the press to my advantage.

Nobody finishes reading the daily articles about low-level street murders. Nobody listens to the newslady on T.V. telling us again about bullets flying through the doors in poor neighborhoods. But the murder of an old white rich woman, in her home, in a tourist town, with missing jewelry, that's a different story. No judge expecting to be reelected would remotely consider the possibility of stepping out on a legal limb.

After Investigator Riley laid the case out in his direct testimony, picture perfect, I had the opportunity to attack the facts. Most of what he said, I already knew. But the further I dug, the more I learned.

"The place was a mess. We're still trying to figure out exactly what's missing. We know the jewelry is gone, and a camera, and some cash, but that's all we know right now."

"A camera?"

"Yes, sir. She apparently was taking pictures that day and was seen with a 35-millimeter camera. We haven't been able to find it."

"Did you locate the instrument used to remove her finger?"

"No, sir. We haven't been able to find whatever was used to remove her finger. Until we get the autopsy report back, I can't really speculate."

"Tell me what items you've taken from the house as evidence, or possible evidence."

"Well, the body was removed, of course. And we've taken the clothes of Ms. Charles. We have photographs of the scene and a videotape. The attic vent was removed from the side of the house and I have it in the evidence locker. I also have the matching brass bookend to the one that's missing."

Randy Riley pulled a list from his file and began reading down the list.

"We collected all the knives in the house to be analyzed for blood, and the big jewelry box where we believe she kept valuables. We are analyzing fingerprints we found throughout the house. The house is still secure as a crime scene. There were some papers found around the body."

"What kind of papers?"

"Letters, documents." There was hesitation in his voice.

"What kind of letters or documents?"

"Well, one of them was a letter from you."

I knew what it was. There was no reason to ask. It was the letter sent several weeks before she was killed. I hinted about my financial problems hoping she would pay me what she owed. I finished the letter with an implied threat of legal action. It did seem strange that she wouldn't have thrown it away or at least put it somewhere.

I felt the eyes of my client glance in my direction before I asked the next question.

"Tell me the names of the people in the neighborhood who you say gave information about a suspicious car."

"Ann Gilbert and Marty Corzine. They both gave written statements."

"Do you have in your possession the videotape allegedly showing my client selling a piece of jewelry?"

"Yes, sir. I have a copy."

"Your Honor, with your permission, I'd like to play that videotape in open court."

"Granted."

We all sat quietly and watched a grainy videotape

filmed from across a motel room. A man identified as
Curt Junkins sat on the couch apparently wired for
sound. There was a knock on the door and Junkins said,
"Come in."

Brad Caine appeared on the videotape dressed
neatly. His voice was sharp and businesslike.

Junkins said, "I'm glad you called. Is the shit any
good?"

Brad answered as he sat down in the chair next to
the couch, "Yes."

I could see Brad Caine on the videotape glance
around the room like a man who doesn't trust the situation. He pulled the necklace from his jacket pocket and
handed it to Curt Junkins. Junkins laid it down on the
coffee table and flipped a jeweler's loupe to his eye. It
looked to be the same necklace Brad showed me at the
diner.

"Where'd you get it?" Junkins asked.

"Never mind. If you've got the money, there might
be more."

It was a bad statement, but it could be explained. As
the tape continued, I hoped we were finished with the
bad statements. Brad had assured me that there was
nothing to hurt him. It was just a videotape of a man
trying to sell a piece of jewelry to a man he knew was in
the jewelry-buying business. A man, unfortunately, Brad
Caine had originally met back in his days of selling items
he had stolen from other people's houses.

"How much more do you have?" Curt Junkins asked.

"Do you want to buy the necklace or not?"

Brad Caine turned his head and looked directly into

the video camera. He seemed itchy and nervous, but who wouldn't be, sitting in a motel room trying to sell jewelry to a guy you knew had stepped back and forth over the legal lines.

Curt Junkins continued to examine the necklace.

"I'll give you fifteen hundred dollars for it."

Brad said, "Why don't you just rob me?"

Money was exchanged. Brad stood up to leave. Curt said, "How do I get in touch with you?"

From off camera, Brad's voice said, "I'll be staying at the Fairfax Inn near the interstate in Loxley."

And then the tape ended. I waited for the bailiff to turn off the television.

"Investigator Riley, when was that tape made?"

"On the Monday night after Ms. Charles was killed on Sunday."

"Why did you wait to arrest Brad Caine until Wednesday?"

"The FBI was the agency working the jewelry sale. They called us to see if the necklace belonged to Haddie Charles. Her sister identified the necklace. We didn't feel like we could wait to set up another sale. We were afraid he might get nervous, dump the jewelry in the bay, or take off."

I raised my voice, "Have you found the rest of the stolen jewelry?"

"No, sir."

I took a jab. "In fact, when you arrested Brad, you didn't find any evidence linking him to Haddie Charles or her murder?"

"We found the fifteen hundred dollars in marked

bills he got from Mr. Junkins."

"But you didn't find any more jewelry, or the camera, or a murder weapon, or a hacksaw, or burglar tools?"

"No, sir, but we did find a pair of rubber gloves hidden in the ceiling of Mr. Caine's motel room. We sent them to be analyzed for blood or fibers. They were wet. They looked recently washed, and Mr. Caine had been staying in the motel room at least two nights."

Brad leaned over and whispered in my ear, "Those aren't mine."

The hearing wound down. The judge bound the case over to the grand jury and refused to set a bond. The D.A.'s office handed me a stack of paperwork and promised more as they got it. Brad Caine was taken back to the jail in shackles while cameramen and reporters asked him questions like, "Did you kill Haddie Charles?" He kept his head up and walked straight.

The next morning I walked in the door of the office to hear Rose announce, "Your lovely daughter Becky called. She's on her way over here."

I looked through my handwritten messages and didn't respond.

"I'll never understand," she said, "why you let them treat you the way they do."

I was only sitting at my desk five minutes when I heard Becky's footsteps in the hall. She barged in as usual and sat down in her oversized coat with her purse wedged between her knees.

"Where is she?"

"I don't know where she is, Becky," I answered.

"She left the rehab. Just walked out the door. Is she staying with you?"

"No, she's not staying with me."

"You're lying. You've seen her."

"I didn't say I haven't seen her. I said she wasn't staying with me."

Becky slammed her hand against the armrest of the chair. "Stop playing games. You're the last person she needs to be seeing. You're the reason she's so screwed up in the first place."

I'd heard it all before.

She yelled, "How can you just sit there and pretend it didn't happen? I saw it. I saw it with my own two eyes."

"Nothing happened, Becky. You can believe what you want to believe. It was an accident. She was just a little girl. I know what it looked like, I know I was drunk, but nothing happened."

"Bullshit." She stood up. "Bullshit, bullshit, bullshit," she screamed. "Why did you have to choose her? She was the youngest. She was the weakest."

Becky sat down in the chair, her face contorted in anger. She yanked off her coat. I pictured Rose sitting at her desk on the other side of the door, listening, trying to piece together what she was hearing along with everything else she'd overheard through the years.

Becky leaned forward and said, "But then again, I guess that's why you picked Kelly, wasn't it? Because she was the youngest. Because she was the weakest. You should be in jail with your clients, with Brad Caine. What you did is worse. At least he killed his victim. You just left yours emotionally crippled. Bouncing around from one man to the next, looking for a father figure. Taking every drug she can find trying to forget what you did to her."

When she stopped talking there was no peace in the silence.

"What do you want from me, Becky?"

Her eyes left mine and wandered around the room like she was talking to herself. "Sometimes I want you just to have the guts to admit what you did. Sometimes I want you to suffer the way other people suffer. But I guess what I really want is for it never to have happened. I wish I hadn't walked in and seen it. I wish there was nothing for me to walk in and see."

The silence returned, and with the silence, Becky's eyes returned to mine.

"Nothing happened, Becky."

"If you don't give a shit about me, or Mark, or Mom, or even yourself, I don't care. But you should at least give a shit what happens to Kelly. Do you? Do you care if she ends up dead in some motel room, or on the side of the highway? Or do you wish she would die so you don't have to think about it every time you see her? Is that what you wish?"

I wanted her to leave. "No, that's not what I want."

"Then call me when you see her. Call me if you hear from her. You're not doing Kelly any favors giving her money or bailing her out over and over again. She's not going to get better by herself. You're not going to turn around one day and find her with a good job, a healthy relationship, or a clean place to live."

"You can't force her to get help, Becky. She won't change until she wants to change."

Becky collected her coat and purse. I was relieved but knew from experience she might throw it all on the floor and start all over again.

She stopped at the door, her face red, emotionally teetering somewhere between rage and tears.

"You're a piece of shit, Daddy."

And then she left. I listened to Becky's footsteps on

the hardwood floor of the hallway. I was glad she was gone. No words or display of emotion from me could shake her hatred. I took a deep breath, picked up the top message on the stack, and returned the call of someone whose name meant nothing to me. No one was home.

CHAPTER 10

I scheduled a meeting in the jail with Brad. I wanted Junior Miflin to join us, but before all three of us got together, I met with Junior alone in a conference room at the courthouse.

"Did you find Edward Polston?"

"No. Nobody seems to know where the hell he went off to. He hasn't been seen around here in almost a year. He's got a few misdemeanor and DUI arrests, but nothin' big. He worked at a gas station near Stapleton, but the last they heard he was workin' offshore in Louisiana or Texas. One guy told me Polston went to South America. I couldn't get anything solid. A buddy in the sheriff's department got me this copy of his bookin' photograph."

He handed me a photograph of a scruffy white man, mid-thirties. It would be effective, blown-up, pinned to the wall in a trial, staring at the jury. I planned to point at the picture and scream a lot about the "real killer." In many ways the photograph and the absence of Edward Polston would be more dramatic and effective than Edward Polston himself. Particularly if we couldn't prove his presence in the county the day Brad met him at

McDonald's. People like Edward Polston drift in and out of places.

"What else did you get for me?"

"Caine pled guilty to burglaries in Birmingham about six years ago. He served two years of his five-year sentence and hasn't been arrested since then. A girl was charged along with him, a co-defendant named Gracie Patrick. She got probation."

"Did you get an address or phone number for Gracie Patrick?"

"Yeah."

He handed me a piece of paper with an address and phone number scrawled in pencil.

Junior Miflin added, "None of my people have heard any word on the street about fancy jewelry. I talked with my pawnshop guys. Nothing out of the ordinary."

"O.K. Let's go over to the jail. I want you to meet the man you're working for."

The three of us sat down in the same room in the jail where I met Brad before. After introductions we got down to business.

"Is this the Edward Polston you know?" I showed Brad Caine the photograph through the screen.

"That's him. Did you find him? He can tell you he gave me the necklace."

"We didn't find him, Brad. He might have gone to Texas or Louisiana. Maybe even South America. Don't be so sure he's gonna help us. If he stole the jewelry, if he's the one who killed the old lady, he won't be easy to find, and besides, if we do find him, he sure as hell isn't going to admit he gave you the necklace on the morning after the woman was killed. How did you get in touch with him?"

"We talked on the phone the week before I came down here. He said he wanted to settle his debt. I told him I was coming down to Baldwin County and Eddie set up the meeting. I think he called from a pay phone."

"Why did he owe you money?"

"A year or so earlier I ran into him, and he needed money bad. I loaned him five hundred dollars. I figured he'd be good for it. Do you think he killed Haddie Charles?"

I answered, "It makes sense, doesn't it? He broke in the house, the lady came home at the wrong time. And then he gave you the necklace and disappeared."

Brad shook his head. "He doesn't seem like the kind of guy who would kill somebody. He seems like the kinda guy who would run."

"Well," I suggested, "maybe you should keep that to yourself."

Junior asked, "Who is Gracie Patrick?"

Brad blinked. "How is she involved?"

"The court file in Birmingham on your burglaries six years ago says she was arrested with you. We just wondered who she is."

Brad seemed to craft his answer carefully. "She was my girlfriend. It was a weird time. I haven't talked to her since that case. She got probation, I went to jail. It probably should have been the other way around."

I spoke. "Brad, I've got a copy of the written statement you gave the cops when you were arrested at the motel room. You wrote, 'I left Birmingham at around ten-thirty or eleven o'clock at night. I drove halfway and slept in my car in a parking lot in Greenville. I drove the rest of the way the next morning and checked into the motel around ten o'clock in the morning. I met Eddie Polston outside the McDonald's in Loxley around ten-thirty. Polston gave me a necklace as payment for money I loaned him. That's all I know.'"

I held the written statement up to the screen. "Is that what you wrote?"

"Yes."

"Did you sign the Miranda Rights form?"

"Yes."

"Brad, it's only a four- or five-hour trip from Birmingham to Loxley. Why would you drive two hours, sleep in your car in Greenville, and then drive the other two hours the next morning? And why would you sleep in your car in the first place?"

Brad lowered his head. I looked at Junior, and he looked at me.

"It was stupid," Brad said. "I was scared. I figured if I told them I wasn't even here yet, I wasn't even in the county, then they'd know I didn't kill Haddie Charles. They told me she was killed Sunday night before I wrote the statement. It was stupid."

"Yes, it was stupid, but we're stuck with it. Where did you spend the night?"

"I left Birmingham late, around eleven at night. I drove straight through. There was no sense paying for the night at a motel, so I just parked my car behind McDonald's and slept. I didn't want anybody to see me so I pulled behind the dumpsters in a place no one would bother me. I checked into the motel about ten o'clock and met with Eddie at ten-thirty. I went through the drive-through at McDonald's, ate in the car, and then showed up at your office."

"Where'd you go after you left my office?"

"I drove around looking for places to rent down in Gulf Shores. Then I met with Junkins."

"Did you drive through the old lady's neighbor-hood?"

"I don't know. I don't know where she lived."

I jotted notes as we spoke and then asked, "What about the rubber gloves?"

"They aren't mine. I don't know where they came from."

I turned to Junior Miflin and proceeded down my list.

"Junior, go to the motel and sniff around. Also, go to McDonald's and find out if any of the employees remember seeing Brad or his car that night. Get a prior history on the jewelry guy, Curt Junkins. And see if those witnesses in the old lady's neighborhood will talk to you about the car they say they saw on Sunday afternoon."

I looked at Brad Caine and said, "Earlier, you said you didn't leave Birmingham until late Sunday night, around eleven o'clock. Haddie Charles was already dead by eleven o'clock. Give me the names of every person in Birmingham who saw you after three or four on Sunday afternoon."

Brad thought out loud, "I ate lunch with a guy named Phillip Ray. I left him at about twelve-thirty and went to my apartment to pack everything into boxes. My phone was already disconnected, so I didn't get any calls. I stayed in the apartment and ate all the leftovers for dinner. When I finally got everything packed up, I stacked the boxes in the living room so they'd be easy to load up when I came back in a few days with a truck. There was no one in the parking lot when I left. It was Sunday night. I drove down alone."

Junior Miflin asked, "Did you stop and get gas somewhere on the way, maybe use a credit card or keep the receipt?"

Brad shook his head. "I got gas the day before in Birmingham, and then I filled up again the day before I got arrested, which was Tuesday."

The meeting ended. I stepped outside with Junior, and we stood together while he lit a cigarette.

"Bad luck," Junior said.

"What do you mean?"

"Bad luck he didn't get gas on the way down, or someone didn't stop by and see him at his apartment while he was packing."

I added, "Bad luck, or he's lying."

Junior took a long draw on his cigarette. The smoke flowed back out through his nose. Who was the first man to find value in the process of inhaling the smoke of a leaf? I almost asked Junior for a cigarette. The words ran from my mind to my tongue, as close as words can get without actually coming out to be heard. Junior took another drag. The red end brightened, and I could almost feel the warm smoke flow down into my lungs, the soft lightness in my head, and then the flow back through the channel and outside again.

He dropped the cigarette on the sidewalk and swiveled the sole of his shoe on the butt. Junior said, "I don't think this one is lying. That's what my gut tells me. I'll call you in a few days."

CHAPTER 11

Sitting alone in my office one evening, after a few drinks, I called the number for Gracie Patrick.

"Hello."

"May I speak to Gracie Patrick?"

There was silence on the line like Gracie was weighing the possibility that I was a bill collector. I knew the feeling and said out loud, "I'm not a bill collector."

"Then who are you?" she asked.

"My name is Jack Skinner. I'm a lawyer down in Baldwin County. You pass by my office on the way to the beach in Gulf Shores. I represent Brad Caine."

There was another skip in the conversation. The line was quiet for a moment before Gracie Patrick said, "What kind of trouble has he gotten himself into?"

"Well, it isn't good. He's accused of killing a lady during a burglary."

Another moment of silence passed.

"What did you say your name was?"

"Jack Skinner."

"Mr. Skinner, I wouldn't doubt he did it. I wouldn't doubt anything Brad Caine has done."

"Why do you say that?" I took a quiet sip of whiskey, careful not to rattle the cubes.

"If you're callin' me, you already know we were arrested together. You already know we had burglary cases. I've done my probation. I've got a halfway decent life now."

"Did Brad ever hurt anybody in those burglaries in Birmingham?"

"I guess that depends on what you mean by hurt," she said.

"Did anybody get injured?"

"Nobody was home at the houses we broke into. They were empty. But he hurt me. He almost ruined my life."

"How's that?" I asked.

"I was all strung out on drugs. I would've crawled on my knees over broken glass for a painkiller or a rock of crack. He knew that. He used it. We would drive through neighborhoods and he'd send me up to knock on the doors, see if anybody was home. It was my face people would see when they opened their doors, and I'd make up some stupid story about looking for a person who didn't exist."

Her voice had the sound of a person recalling a time far away. A time better left unremembered.

"How did you get caught?"

"I was standing at a door, making up a story, and I just started crying. I stood in front of a stranger, and just cried, with my back to Brad sitting in the car in the driveway. He must have seen something was wrong. He left. He just drove away and left me there. I told the police everything. I told 'em about every single burglary I could remember, and about Brad, and how he crawled through the side attic vents, and wore a service uniform, and pretended he was checking the cable. I told 'em about the drugs, and the money, and the jewelry. He only pled guilty because I agreed to testify."

I had never seen Gracie Patrick, but I could picture her. Small, pretty, big sad eyes. Grew up believing the world would take care of her, and when it didn't, she found herself pushed around by the cross-currents of this life. Helpless to her weaknesses, blind to her strengths.

"You asked me if anyone was hurt. I was hurt. The people who owned the houses were hurt. And I suppose Brad was hurt. He went to prison."

I waited for her to continue.

"No, Mr. Skinner, I never saw him hit anyone. Brad always preferred to talk his way out, or tell lies until no one could find the truth. I loved him. It seems stupid now. But I was in love with him. Between Brad and the drugs, I would have done anything for him. I just couldn't stop crying when that lady came to the door. She looked like my mother, with a blue apron. The house smelled like cookies. My mother used to make cookies. She took me by the hand and sat me down on her couch while she called the police. I remember, she actually gave me a cookie. I sat on the couch with the lady whose house we planned to burglarize eating a cookie. Can you believe that?"

I silently refilled my whiskey glass.

"Gracie, what kind of uniform did he wear?"

"It was just a gray uniform with a name patch. We

always used to laugh at the name: Arnold. Brad didn't look much like an Arnold."

"Have you ever heard of Haddie Charles, Edward Polston, or Curt Junkins?"

"I've heard of Curt Junkins. I don't know the other two. Curt used to buy stolen jewelry from Brad. I only saw him once, but I heard Brad talking to him on the telephone lots of times."

"Did Brad wear gloves?"

"I almost never went inside the houses. After I made sure no one was home, Brad would get his extension ladder out of the back of the wagon, crawl through into the attic, do whatever he did to the alarm if they had one, drop down into the house, fill up his toolbox, and then come back out the attic side vent. Sometimes, if they had no alarm, or he wanted to take something too big to fit in the toolbox, he'd call me inside. There's a lot of things I don't remember. I had to get screwed up to have the nerve to go."

I asked my question again, "Did he wear gloves, Gracie?"

"I think so, sometimes."

"What kind?"

"I don't really remember. It's been a long time."

"Is there anything else he did in the houses? Something unique to Brad?"

We once again reached a pause. There was something she wasn't saying.

"What is it, Gracie?"

"Sometimes," she said, "Brad would call me in the house. He'd make me do oral sex with him in the middle of the people's living room. In the middle of a burglary. It was weird. I guess he got off on the excitement, the chance of getting caught."

I could hear the embarrassment in her voice. She began to speak almost like she was talking to herself.

"He always promised me the drugs. Always. We would drive straight from the houses to the guy we bought the drugs from. It was my reward. I watched a show the other day on one of those cable channels. They did a study with rats. If the rat pulled the lever on the right, he'd get food and water. If the rat pulled the lever on the left, he'd get cocaine. They showed that rat keep pulling the lever on the left, over and over, until he starved to death."

She was a talker. I think I could've put the phone down, gone to Buddy's for a cheeseburger, and come back to the phone before she noticed I was gone. Instead, I just imagined going to Buddy's, and I sat there and listened to Gracie Patrick. She may have been away from Brad Caine for six years, and maybe away from drugs, but she was in fragments. If I stayed on the phone long enough there was the potential to swing from one emotion to another, sentence by sentence.

I interrupted, "Thanks for your time, Miss Patrick."

"I won't testify for him."

"I didn't ask you to."

"I won't do it. Don't ask me. And please don't call here again."

I waited for her to hang up. We were adrift in silence once again.

"Miss Patrick, are you still there?"

"Yes," she answered.

"Is there anything else you want to say?"

"No."

"Good-bye."

"Good-bye, Mr. Skinner."

CHAPTER 12

I woke up in the pitch black, covered in the fog of alcohol. There was a strange flapping sound coming from somewhere in the room. My first confused thought was wondering where I was. When I grasped the idea I was on my own couch I reached my hand to the place I hoped the lamp would be and flicked on the light. I had fallen asleep in my shirt and tie and at the end of the couch I could see my brown shoes still on my feet. I lifted my heavy body into an upright sitting position, adjusting my eyes toward the corner of the room. A bird flapped and fell, feathers flying in the air. Echo pounced, paws forward, pinning the creature against the wall.

I rubbed my head.

"How the hell'd you get in here?" I said to the cat.

At my feet on the floor a voice said, "The door was unlocked."

There was a delay as my mind processed the information, and then my body shook from the surprise of not being alone.

Kelly's head rested on her arm like a pillow. She said, "What's the matter, Daddy?"

"How'd you get in here?" I repeated, this time to Kelly.

"I told you. The door was unlocked."

"There's a bird in the room."

I pointed, and we both looked. Echo held the brown bird in her mouth, waiting for God knows what. The bird waited also.

I stood and walked to the door, opening it wide for the cat to see. I couldn't think of anything else and resorted to reason.

"Please, Echo. Could you please take the bird back outside?"

There was no immediate response. Kelly sat up on the floor.

I continued, "I appreciate the bird. I appreciate the hard work it must have taken to catch the bird and bring it here, but I'd really like the bird to be outside, please."

Echo dropped her catch, walked into the kitchen, eventually stretching out on the cool linoleum. The bird sat still for a moment, looked around the room, and took off, flying smack into the wall on the other side of the room, bouncing backwards, and then flying into the window. The cat didn't move. She didn't even glance up.

I grabbed the towel off the back of the couch, noticed the clock said 3:22 a.m., and proceeded to chase the bird around the living room in my shirt and tie, my big brown shoes stomping like a baboon. I got him in a corner, and the bird squeaked under the towel like I'd squeezed the life from his tiny body. I ran to the door and hurled the bird and the towel together into the night, closing the door without waiting to see if he flew away.

I went back and sat down on the couch. My head pounded and my heart seemed to be pumping too much blood under too much pressure to all the wrong locations. Kelly had her head back down on her arm. Her glazed eyes looked up at me.

"What are you doing here, Kelly? Have you talked to your sister?"

"I'm tired of talking to my sister. I'm tired." Her words trailed away.

We sat for a moment.

Kelly spoke softly, "You're always here for me, Daddy."

She was barefoot. Her blue jeans were well-worn and the shirt was one I'd never seen before. Kelly's body seemed long stretched across the rug. I turned away.

Out of habit I said, "Kelly, this can't go on forever. You're not a kid anymore. Why can't you just get a job?"

"I don't know, Daddy. Sometimes I wish I was like other people, but I'm not. I can't seem to find a place."

We were quiet for awhile. I watched the cat, her eyes lazily drooping and then opening again. She seemed to have forgotten the bird that hung from her mouth just minutes earlier. I wondered if the bird had forgotten. What a wonderful gift. The cat had no recollection of what she had lost, and the bird had no memory of the horror. They had already moved along, driven forward by a dull desire, unburdened.

Kelly whispered, "How's your case going with that boy they arrested for killing Haddie Charles?"

I was relieved by the change of subject.

"We're still months from trial, but I'm thinking

about filing a speedy trial motion. The longer they have to fish around, the more they're liable to find. If we went to trial tomorrow, it would be a toss-up. I think we've got a shot."

"All my life I've been reading about you in the newspaper, or hearing your stories about cases, but I've never actually seen you in court. I'd like to go sometime, just to watch. They say you're good."

I imagined standing before a jury, turning my head to gather thoughts, and seeing my daughter sitting in the courtroom staring back at me. Secrets are like cancer, tucked away in some little hole, pea-sized and forgotten until they grow, eat away the good things.

The room was silent. At 3:41 in the morning almost no one has a reason to be busy. The late people have found their way home, and the early people aren't quite up yet. I listened for the sound of a car, or a voice in the parking lot, or a television through the thin apartment walls. There was nothing. I tried not to move. It made me remember when Kelly was a tiny baby, patting her back in the crib until she was finally still, and then not moving a muscle in fear she would stir with any sound.

I looked back at Kelly on the floor. Her eyes were closed and her breathing was steady. I stayed awake until the light came through the window, without stirring, afraid her eyes would open with any sound I might make.

CHAPTER 13

I met with Junior Miflin on a Friday morning at the Waffle House. His eyes jumped around from one face to the next.

"Who you lookin' for?"

"No one," Junior said, and stared down at the menu.

I sipped cold coffee. "Is there someone here, in the Waffle House, makin' you nervous?"

"No."

The waitress approached, ugly and haggard. Hair on her face. One look at the woman was enough to understand why she'd never ventured beyond this kind of place.

Junior Miflin ordered a large chocolate milk and french fries. He pulled a piece of paper from his back pocket and began to tell me things.

"I couldn't find anybody at McDonald's who remembered Caine or his car. Nobody remembered seeing a car parked behind the dumpsters, but that don't mean it wasn't there. There's trees back there, and you'd have to go lookin' at nighttime to see a car. I took some pictures. Day and night."

I examined the photographs. Junior's chocolate milk

and golden fries arrived at our table. When the sea-hag waitress bent down to deliver the plate of fries, I saw Junior look down her shirt and steal a peek at her chicken-skin tits.

"You married, Junior?" I asked.

"Yeah."

He took a sip of his milk and began to speak again. There was a thin brown liquid mustache across his top lip.

"Curt Junkins, the jewelry guy. He's been around the block a few times. It looks like maybe he was servin' time in the system with Caine. They might've known each other before, but they weren't ever arrested together.

"Junkins got popped by the Feds in a big sting with about ten other guys, tax evasion and fraud. They kept his indictment secret and got him wired up to pop a few other guys. Caine just came along at the wrong time. He wasn't their target. He just called to unload the necklace and stepped into the shit."

As he talked, Junior munched fries and darted his bat eyes around the Waffle House. He would occasionally look back at the paper unfolded next to his plate. A drop of ketchup landed on the piece of paper, and Junior wiped it off with his finger.

"The witnesses in the old lady's neighborhood can't describe the driver of the car, but they're both pretty consistent with the description of the car: faded red, older model, four-door, driving around slowly. One woman even got the first three numbers of the tag, and they match with Caine's. It's a pretty common car though, and neither witness called the police or anything. This Ann Gilbert is a busybody. You'll eat her ass for lunch on the witness stand."

The french fries were nearly gone, and I was glad. There were just a few left, scattered like small greasy logs on the plate around a pool of red ketchup.

"Anything else, Junior?"

"I went down to the motel. Caine checked in like he said, Monday morning around ten. He paid cash for one night, and then paid cash on Tuesday for the next night. Nobody remembers much about him. One maid remembers knocking on his door Tuesday morning to clean the room. Caine told her to come back later. The maid said she thought someone else was in the room with him, but never saw anybody."

The last crispy blackish fry was alone in the center of the white plate. Junior churned down the final swallow of thick chocolate milk. He handed me the piece of paper with the ketchup stain and dug through his bulky brown wallet as he stood. Junior dropped a five dollar bill on the table.

"Let me know what you need next," he said, and left.

I drove directly to the jail to see Brad Caine. We took our usual positions across from one another in the tiny room. Brad was anxious.

"I'd really like to get outta here, Jack. I'm gettin' a bad feeling about this. These people are under a lot of pressure to find whoever killed that old lady. I'm all they've got."

He shook his head and said slowly, "I can't go back to prison. You just don't know what it's like. You've got no idea. Do you know some of the shit I saw in there? Do you?" He slid up to the front of his chair, face against the screen.

"No, Brad. I don't," I said.

"Well, I'll tell you. I saw a man shove his fist completely up the ass of another man. I saw it, I heard him yell like his guts were on fire. I saw a Mexican guy get cut from his throat to his bellybutton. It opened up like a hole in the sky. I just stood there and watched it."

He waited for me to react. I didn't.

"Brad, you've got to be patient. Junior's been out seeing people. I can file a speedy trial motion. You're in jail, this is a capital case, we've got priority. Unless the State's got a good reason, they won't get a continuance, but we're not ready yet. The jail is full of guys who got in too big of a hurry going to trial."

Brad took a deep breath and seemed to relax a bit.

"Did you ever have anyone in the motel room with you in Loxley, at any time?"

"Who told you that?"

"Brad. Listen to my question. Every time we meet, every time we speak, you've got to be learning about this case. The evidence they have, what the witnesses will say, how to testify in case you get on the witness stand. Listen to my question. Did you ever have anyone in the motel room with you in Loxley, at any time?"

"No."

"Is there any reason a maid would say you did?"

"A maid came to the door, but I was alone. I just wasn't dressed yet. It was Tuesday morning. I told her to come back later."

And then he added, "What do you mean 'in case' I

get on the witness stand? Don't you think I need to testify, to tell the jury I didn't do it?"

"It depends. We won't make that decision until we have to. I've watched innocent people talk themselves into a conviction on the witness stand. We'll have to see how the case is going before we decide."

He seemed satisfied.

"How long have you had your car?"

"Almost two years."

"Did you let anyone borrow it while you were down here?"

"No."

"Is there any way those people in Haddie Charles's neighborhood saw your car that Sunday?"

"No way. It wasn't my car they saw."

I made a note to have Junior do a search in the computer for similar cars registered in the state with similar first numbers on the tag.

"Did you know Curt Junkins before prison?"

"Yeah. We met when I was sellin' the stolen jewelry from my Birmingham burglaries years ago. He ended up in prison for something completely different. I never saw him inside."

Brad watched me write. He asked, "Do you believe left-handed people are different somehow? I mean, besides being left-handed."

"I don't know, Brad. Maybe."

He said, "My grandmother told me I started out right-handed, but my father made me do everything with my left hand because he wanted me to be a baseball player. It's supposed to be an advantage in baseball.

Being left-handed. But I wouldn't know. I never played baseball."

We looked at each other a moment.

"What did you wear when you broke into the houses in Birmingham?"

Brad didn't hesitate. "A gray service uniform. It had a name tag sewed on. I figured if anyone came home while I was inside, I could talk my way out. Just say I was checkin' the cable T.V., there's a problem in this area, or some shit like that. If you sound like you know what you're talkin' about, and you stand your ground, people will believe almost anything. Nobody ever came home though."

"How'd you get caught?"

"Gracie. She melted down. I don't blame her. We would've gotten caught eventually. It's not like we were gonna just stop ourselves and get regular jobs."

Brad Caine smiled and said to himself, "It was crazy."

"I'm sure the prosecution will try to show that the burglary down here was the same operation as your burglaries in Birmingham. Entrance through the attic, jewelry stolen, jewelry taken straight to Curt Junkins. They'll try to make a big deal out of that."

"I never killed anybody in Birmingham. And I had someone with me, Gracie, who knocked on the doors, stood lookout. It wasn't the same."

"No, it wasn't."

Our conversation ended. I stayed in the room a few minutes alone after they led Brad away. He was consistent. He didn't know I'd talked to Gracie. He didn't know I already knew he sold stolen jewelry to Junkins before, or used a uniform in the Birmingham burglaries, or how he got caught. After a few coaching sessions, Brad Caine would make a good witness. He had that certain air of believability. He had the frustration of an innocent man.

CHAPTER 14

I got a call from the district attorney's office letting me know the autopsy and preliminary forensics reports had arrived. When I went in to see Deborah Webb again, she handed me a large yellow envelope.

Deborah said, "I haven't had a chance to pick it apart yet, but basically it looks like she was hit on the right side of her head, temple area, with something hard. The injury matches the brass bookend left behind. She probably died quick."

"And they never found the other bookend?"

"No."

"Fingerprints?"

"No. Nothing that can be used. But we knew that after the gloves were found in your boy's motel room. He used gloves in the Birmingham burglaries. By the way, I'll be filing a motion for pretrial determination of the admissibility of evidence so we can introduce the Birmingham burglaries. Gloves, entrance through the attic, jewelry, selling the jewelry to Mr. Junkins."

"Do we know our judge yet?" I asked.

"No. The indictment will be processed tomorrow. I'll

give you a copy. We've got a count for capital murder-burglary first degree, and a count for capital murder-robbery first degree, just in case the jury thinks your boy intended to wait for Ms. Charles."

Deborah looked a bit puzzled and added, "There's nothing in Caine's history to make me think he killed before. I've still got my doubts he was alone, but if he's not talkin', I guess we'll never know. The finger thing is kinda weird. I guess he couldn't slip it off and just wouldn't walk away from that big diamond."

I listened. It's the hardest lesson for a lawyer to learn. When to shut up and listen.

"I know it's early, Jack, and I think our case is pretty strong, but if your boy had an accomplice, or he could help recover the family jewelry, we might be able to take death off the table. It's a high-profile case, but I doubt the family of Haddie Charles would give us a lot of grief if Caine pleaded and we recommended life without parole. Her crazy sisters seem more concerned with getting back the jewelry than anything else."

I thumbed through the pages of the autopsy report and said, "I disagree."

"With what?"

"With your assessment that the case is strong. If the case was strong, you'd never take death off the table. This could be a feather in your boss's cap."

Deborah smiled. "Everybody thinks you're such a tough guy, but I know you agonize over these cases. I know you'll talk to Mr. Caine about my offer and let him decide his own fate."

She was right. One of the forensics reports noted

hairs found.

"Did you find some hairs?"

"Yes. None match Brad Caine. We found two near the body. Brown. Long. Probably from a woman. They could belong to anyone, from the cleaning lady to the real estate agent who found the body."

"Or to the real killer," I added.

"I'm sure you'll make a big show out of the hairs, but you better be careful. Out of one side of your mouth you'll be telling the jury that Edward Polston is the murderer, and out of the other side you'll be screaming about a mystery woman with long brown hair."

I pretended to be busy reading the report, but I heard every word she said.

"Deborah, just a heads-up, Mr. Caine will probably ask me to file a speedy trial motion. We're gonna hold your feet to the fire."

She held her face well, but Deborah was surprised. As I stood to leave she announced, "You know what they say, the prison is full of men whose lawyers announced ready for trial."

The very point I had recently made to Brad. I walked from the courthouse to the jail to meet again with Brad.

I asked him, "Edward Polston, his hair in the picture looks black. Was it always black?"

Brad shook his head, "Yes." And then asked, "Why?"

"They found a few long brown hairs around the dead woman's body. Probably female. They didn't find any of your hair, or fingerprints, or anything else."

"There's no way they could. I've never been in the

lady's house."

"The D.A.'s office will be filing a motion for the pre-trial determination of the admissibility of evidence. That means they're asking the judge to be allowed to introduce evidence to the jury of your Birmingham burglaries because they fit a common scheme or plan. Usually a defendant's prior crimes are inadmissible except to attack your credibility if you testify, but if the court grants their motion, the jury will hear about how in the past you've broken into a residence, climbing through the side attic vent, for the purpose of stealing jewelry, wearing gloves, and then selling the stolen jewelry to Curt Junkins. Their whole case could hinge on that motion, but with the state of the law now, and our conservative judges, they've got a good chance of having the court rule in their favor."

Brad thought a moment and answered, "That doesn't seem real fair. I mean, I've already pled guilty in those other cases. I did my time. Most other burglars steal jewelry. Most other burglars wear gloves. And all I did was take a necklace to a guy I knew six or seven years ago."

"In Birmingham, why did you break in through the side attic vent?"

Brad Caine shrugged, "Well, if somebody comes home, and I've broken in through a window or door, there's no explanation, there's no way to talk my way out. I never carried a weapon. But if you enter through the gable vent, just pop out a few nails, people will think I'm just a serviceman, just there to check the cable. Besides, some of the alarm systems are located in the attic. Two or three times I had alarms go off. I'd just climb down the ladder with my toolbox, wave to the neighbors, and drive away."

"If you testify, Brad, there's a thin line to walk. You've got to be believable. You've got to look those people in the eye and say, 'I've made mistakes. I've done stupid things. But I never killed anybody. I never hurt anybody, ever. And I wouldn't do it. The whole reason I went through the attics in Birmingham was to avoid the possibility of a confrontation.'"

Brad jotted notes on his pad. I noticed at the top of the paper he wrote "*Testimony.*"

I continued, "Over the next several months we'll work on how to testify. One answer, one wrong answer, could make all the difference. One reaction, or facial expression. That's all it takes."

"O.K.," he said, and wrote down a word I couldn't read.

"Brad, we need to talk about something. Don't give me an answer now, just think about it. Part of my job is to create options for you in this process. Deborah Webb hinted at the possibility of a plea bargain. In exchange for you identifying your accomplice, if you had one, and helping to recover the stolen family jewelry, they would recommend life without parole. They'd take the death penalty out of the equation."

Brad had a blank look on his face.

"Mr. Skinner, if you don't believe in me, say so right now. Just say so. Because I can't go into the trial of my life with a lawyer who thinks I'm guilty. I'd rather do it alone."

"I never said I didn't believe you, Brad. I never said that."

"How could you expect me to consider pleading guilty to something I didn't do in exchange for providing information or jewelry I don't have? And then spending the rest of my life in prison?"

I raised my voice. "I've been doin' this shit a long time. You've got no idea. But I'll tell you this, part of my job is to communicate to you plea offers. You can take 'em or leave 'em, but it doesn't have a goddamned thing to do with what I believe or don't believe."

I took a deep breath and leaned back in the chair. There was no room for Brad Caine to misunderstand my anger at his challenge.

"Sorry," he whispered. "I'm sorry."

I was tired, ready to go home.

"What about the speedy trial motion?" he asked.

"Well, I think it's a good idea. Keep 'em back on their heels. They're liable to find some bored housewife in the neighborhood who has seen your picture in the paper and decides she saw you on the day of the murder. If you want me to file it, I will."

"I want you to file it."

I gathered my papers to leave. There was a sickly food smell in the jail. My stomach was heavy.

CHAPTER 15

I gave Kelly a key to my apartment. For a few weeks she came and went. Out of habit I hid everything valuable. Through the years Kelly had stolen anything in plain sight to trade or sell for drugs. I often wondered how strong the feeling must be. A person who has never felt the warmth of heroin can stand righteous and proclaim control over the temptations of sin. But that same person, wrapped in the blanket of the drug, and then unwrapped to face the cold, would shove a hand into the purse of her dying mother and steal her last dollar bill.

Are those people predestined to fail? Are they the weak members of the Darwinian herd, bound to seek and find the turns in the maze leading to hell? Or can any of us be pulled along by the strings of the devil in search of the satisfaction of the needle?

I came home to find Kelly on the couch watching cartoons. She was wearing one of my large sweatshirts and slowly pulled a pillow into her lap to cover her underwear. I hung my jacket across the back of a chair, fixed a drink, and sat down in the same chair on the far side of the couch. Kelly had her back to the door and didn't turn from the T.V. as Echo wedged her head into the crack of the open door and came inside with the squeak of the hinge, leaving a gap of six inches.

"I love cartoons," she said.

The drink was cool to my lips. I took a big sip, and another, before setting the glass on my knee.

"What did you do today?" I asked.

"This," Kelly answered.

"All day? You watched cartoons?"

"Yes."

We watched together.

I asked, "Does that roadrunner ever get caught?"

Kelly turned and looked at me for the first time. She answered quickly, "No. He never does." She turned back to the show. I saw the dark circles underneath her eyes. There wasn't much to talk about. There was no discomfort in the silence, but that's only because the glazed look on Kelly's face made me wonder if she remembered I was even in the room.

The door busted wide open and slammed against the wall. The sudden movement was startling, and I dropped the glass from my knee. It landed on the carpet and shot ice cubes and whiskey against the ugly brown chair. I looked up to see Becky in the doorway.

"I knew it," Becky said. "I knew she was staying here." Her tongue was sharp with spite.

I fought back. "It's better than sleeping in a ditch."

"No," she said. "It's not. Kelly sleeping in the apartment with her sick father, the man who molested her, is not better than sleeping in a ditch. It's not better than sleeping anywhere."

Kelly never moved her gaze from the stupid coyote. Becky left the door open, marched across the room, and sat her big ass on the couch next to Kelly. They say animals can tell a storm is on the way by the change in pressure. Echo left the room in a hurry. I didn't have the energy to follow.

I picked up the glass from the carpet and turned it upright. It was empty. The precious gold liquid was gone, and I swiveled on the dilemma of sitting still or making my way back to the kitchen for a refill.

Becky spoke. "Well, here we are. One big happy family sitting around the living room. Isn't it wonderful. I think it's wonderful."

Becky rolled Kelly's arm looking for needle marks. Becky turned to me and said, "Why is she in her underwear? Why is she sitting on your couch while you get drunk, wearing your shirt, in her underwear? Why? How many drinks does it take to wash away inhibitions? I'm just curious. I'd like to know."

Kelly stared at the television. The coyote leaned out over the ledge of a cliff and fell forever down a mountain. He landed with a thud and a puff of dust. Becky had melted into a strange mood. She was calm.

"Why don't you admit what you did? Just face it?"

"I didn't do anything," I answered calmly.

Becky continued, "Well let's say, just for the sake of argument, that you did. You molested your five-year-old daughter. And got caught. What would you do now, all these years later? What would you do?"

It was a trick question, of course. I'd seen it used in the courtroom. I'd even used it before. I surprised myself and answered anyway.

"I don't know. I guess I'd start by apologizing. Then I'd get some help. Try to fix the problem. But I'm not a child molester, so I don't know what a child molester would do."

Becky smiled and shook her head. "I get it. You're trying to argue that just because you did it one time, you're not really a 'child molester.' You're just a guy who got drunk and did something stupid, or did it happen more than once?"

Becky spoke further. "But when you kill somebody, Dad, murder somebody, even just once, you're always a murderer. For the rest of your life you're a murderer. Like your client, Brad Caine. He'll always be a murderer, whether he's convicted or not, whether he kills again or not. Just like you'll always be a child molester, whether you admit to it or not, or touch another little girl. It doesn't matter."

The words flew around the room like stones swung on ropes, just above my head. They were hard and flew with purpose. From the side I could see tears rolling quietly down Kelly's face. I hoped she was crying for the coyote. I hoped, at least for this day, Kelly had succeeded in burning away the edges of her brain with the drugs, causing a hard crusty wall between her mind and the outside world.

We all just sat in that despicable little room and waited. Finally Becky asked, "Is this the worst conversation you've ever had?"

I thought about it and answered, "It's in the top five."

Becky turned her eyes to the cartoon. I eventually turned also. The three of us watched the coyote place a load of dynamite behind a big boulder. He strung a line back behind a tree and waited. The roadrunner came hauling ass down the road, stopped next to the boulder, and looked around. The coyote seized the opportunity and pushed down the handle of the bomb box, but nothing happened. The roadrunner made a 'beep' sound and took off around the corner. The coyote tiptoed to the place in the road by the boulder, scratched his old tired head, and then the dynamite exploded, rolling the big boulder into the road and flattening the coyote.

Kelly pushed a button on the remote control and the television turned off. She continued to stare at the screen. The three of us sat quietly for a very long time. All the best stories are told in silence.

Without warning, Becky stood and began to collect Kelly's belongings. There wasn't much to collect. I turned my head away as my youngest daughter pulled up her blue jeans, her back toward me. As they walked through the open door without a word, Echo darted inside with a small green lizard wiggling side to side in her mouth. It seemed pointless to move from my spot, so I didn't. Echo dropped the lizard and the green creature ran haphazard toward the kitchen and under the refrigerator. I wondered briefly how many disoriented animals found themselves, weak and lost, in the great lizard graveyard underneath my favorite appliance?

CHAPTER 16

Weeks went by. I had other clients, but my mind always came to rest on Brad Caine. There were times I felt sure Brad was not guilty, and the weight of the world rested on my shoulders. There were other times I felt Brad gently guide me in one direction or another, with the touch of a master manipulator. I genuinely could not get a tight grip around the entire case.

People outside the criminal justice system often asked me, "How do you represent a guilty person?" It's never so simple. Most times a lawyer never really knows. We weren't there. We didn't know the people before the event. And even a guilty man deserves enthusiastic representation. Without such representation, we could never weed out the innocent. William Shakespeare wrote, "First, kill all the lawyers," or something like that. In the context of the story in which he wrote such a sentence, killing all the lawyers was intended to destroy the first line of defense of the common man against the state. People are innocent until proven guilty, not the other way around. It's impossible to truly understand until it's your ass on the line, or your son's, or best friend's, or your client's.

Rose brought me a stack of bills, unopened. My accountant called. The IRS was losing patience. There was still back child support owed from years gone by. Tax penalties. Interest. It wasn't hard to see how a man could put a gun to his head and bring it to a stop. If nothing else, there would be pleasure in knowing the tax man wouldn't get another fuckin' dime out of me. But I suppose there was something buried deep in my DNA that wouldn't let me give up. I just kept working.

Brad Caine's file had grown fat with stacks of reports, and photographs, and papers. In the middle of the file I found a copy of the letter I had written Haddie Charles demanding my money. It was a photocopy and around the top of the letter were black spots and splotches where dried blood appeared on the original. Deborah Webb hadn't mentioned the letter in any of our conversations. It was professional courtesy. I suppose my financial problems weren't exactly a secret. I made a note to myself to remember to ask Deborah not to introduce the letter into evidence in the trial. There was no need for the jury to know that Brad's lawyer was hard up for money.

In the color photograph of Haddie's body I could see the letter, face up, just a few inches from her hand with the missing finger. There were other papers and books around her body as if there had been a struggle, as much of a struggle as the old lady could muster before her head was bashed in. Her eyes were closed and her mouth was open. There was a blood stain under her head and another blood stain under her hand. One shoe was off and the other was on. One thing for sure, the photo-graph would piss off a jury. A man's home is his castle. She was killed in her home. In her living room, on her peach-colored carpet. It must have shocked the hell out of the real estate lady.

There were other pictures. The safe in the closet was left wide open. The attic ladder was down. Most of the home was in perfect order. The burglar seemed to know exactly what he was after. Because of the court case between the sisters, plenty of people could have known the old lady had a load of jewelry. From the looks of things, Haddie Charles just came home at the wrong time and probably surprised the killer. Next to her body was a phone on the floor, knocked from the table, off the hook. Maybe she tried to call for help. Maybe the burglar felt he had no choice. Hit her in the head. Then cleaned up carefully after himself, but couldn't resist the big dia-mond on her finger. It seemed strange that a man sur-prised in the act of a burglary, in a panic, would stop and take the time to saw the woman's finger off her hand. The autopsy indicated the cut was jagged, like a hacksaw or serrated knife was used. But whatever was used to cut off her finger, it was taken away, along with the murder weapon itself.

Haddie Charles didn't have close friends, so no one could tell whether there were other items missing from the house. Had the burglar brought the knife or hacksaw with him? Or did he use one from the house? How long did he risk staying in the house looking for jewelry? Did he know Haddie Charles lived alone and no one else would be coming home?

Most importantly, how could Brad Caine know these things if he was only in Baldwin County a short time before the murder?

The district attorney's office did indeed file their motion to introduce evidence of the similar burglaries of Brad Caine in Birmingham. I filed a stack of motions myself to suppress Brad's statement, the gloves found in the motel room, the videotape of the jewelry sale. There was no hope my motions would succeed, but they had to be filed to protect the record for an appeal in the event the jury found Brad guilty. The prosecutor's case was a circumstantial house of cards. If one piece of evidence could be removed, it might all fall apart.

Rose went home for the day. I felt guilty that she hadn't been paid in two weeks, but not guilty enough to return the unopened new bottle of whiskey in my bottom drawer. I sat alone in the silence, the phone finally still. I walked to the closet and pulled out the black briefcase. Resting it in front of me, I rubbed my hand on the smooth cool leather and then tried the lock. No luck. There was a three-digit combination lock. I tried a few random numbers. No luck. And then I shook the case.

It was heavy. Maybe it was full of money. I thought, maybe, if Brad Caine was convicted and sentenced to die, the briefcase would be mine, and everything inside. I imagined stacks of crisp hundred-dollar bills, with thin red paper wrappers around the middle of each stack. Enough to pay all the bills piled on the corner of my desk. Enough to pay Rose, and the tax man, and get a clean start.

I shook the case again. My mind flowed with the whiskey. Maybe it was full of Haddie Charles's jewelry, and a hacksaw. Over a million dollars worth of jewelry. Or maybe it was just papers and personal items. Stupid documents about a sports bar, a bank loan, tax returns. All the shit we accumulate in our lives. Maybe he had an old picture of his mother, his birth certificate, a checkbook. Maybe I didn't want to know what was inside.

I leaned over and placed my nose against the leather. The smell reminded me of something a long time ago. Something good, but I couldn't bring it back. Above the combination lock was a place where initials had probably been. Just a little indentation where the small metal letters had been removed. I put the case back in its place in the closet and finished my glass of whiskey. I was in no hurry to go home, afraid maybe Kelly had come back to the apartment with her crazy sister not far behind.

That coyote didn't have it so bad. Why did he want the roadrunner anyway? What the hell would he do with it? Eat it? It was just a bony bird, all feathers and beak. No. He didn't want to eat it. He just wanted to kill the son-of-a-bitch. Blow his bird bones apart. Stand over the pieces of the carcass and say, "Ah-ha, who got who?"

I would say to the coyote, "Don't waste your time. The satisfaction will never be enough. Better to just go away. Find something else to do."

But I guess it's none of my business.

CHAPTER 17

The night before the hearing on the pending motions, I had a dream. The line between the dream and the real world blurred to no line at all.

I was sitting on the couch in the living room in the house where I was raised, maybe five or six years old, staring across the room at my father in his big chair. He always sat in the same chair in the living room when he got home from work, usually with the newspaper, sometimes watching a television show. There were no sounds except the rustle of the newspaper as my father turned the pages.

In the dream I could see myself on the couch, hands crossed in my lap, shoes and short pants nice and neat. I could feel the warmth and comfort from my childhood, the knowledge of my mother and sisters somewhere in or around the house. A pretty day out the window.

My father continued to read the paper, the top of his head barely visible over the headlines. I wondered what could be in those pages that was so important, but somehow I believed my father's strength and dependability rested in the time he had alone. My mother always demanded our silence during those times, and in my dream, silence existed almost like another person there with us.

I waited. Not nervous or anxious. Just waited. And finally my father folded the paper neatly and placed it on the carpet next to the chair. We sat across the room from each other, staring, until the silence was no longer friendly. I can't explain why.

My father reached his hand to his belt buckle, unfastened the clasp, and pulled the belt from the loops around his waist. I had never been spanked before, not even with an open hand, and had no reason to fear my father or the black belt he held. I watched as he popped the belt across his own knee, testing the pain, measuring the force.

My father stood. A tall man anyway, but a giant to the boy on the couch. Not just a giant physically, but a statue of what a man should be. He walked across the room with big slow steps and stood above me, looking down with his round eyes into the eyes of his own flesh and blood. His arm rose upwards with the thick leather belt high above his head. I felt no fear until I was struck across the face with a power I never imagined existed in this world. The pain was overwhelming and instant. I fell over sideways on the couch, and my father hit me again, and again, and again.

In my dream I saw it from above. His arm swung without mercy, the entire body of the big man behind every blow. The long arm swept in a circle, struck me solid, and then recoiled through a backhand swing. Although I watched it from above, I could feel the pain on my skin and under my shirt. But mostly, I could feel the utter fear of my father and the horror of a world where such a thing could happen. Why would my father hit me?

I woke up, my chest heaving, and sat on the side of the king-size bed. I kept telling myself, "It was just a dream, it was only a dream," until my body believed the truth. I heard a noise behind me and stood. The first thought in my mind was that Echo was in the bed. I flicked on the lamp and stood motionless. Kelly lay asleep on the other side of the bed. She was on her stomach on top of the blankets, naked from the waist up, a pair of white panties covering her rear end.

At that moment I wasn't sure where my dream had started or stopped. It seemed perfectly possible I was still sound asleep. Her clothes were in a pile at the foot of the bed, her key on the side table next to the clock. Kelly's face was turned away and there was the gentle sound of breathing. I took my eyes from the skin of her back and looked at the wall an arm's length to my left. I retreated to the bathroom, locked the door, and stood at the mirror. My face was still the face of the boy in the dream, only bigger, with crow's feet and stubble. My daughter lay in the next room, in my bed, nude. Or had I dreamed it? Dreamed it all?

I unlocked the bathroom door and peeked out into the bedroom. She was there. In a place she shouldn't be. Asleep in my bed. How long had she been there? Was I in the middle of my dream, a boy sitting on the couch with my hands folded in my lap, when she stood at the end of the bed and slowly undressed, dropping her pants, her socks, her shirt, and finally her bra, in the pile on the floor?

I left the bathroom, quickly turned off the lamp on the bedside table, and made my way to the living room. It was almost four a.m. when I made sure the front door was locked. It wasn't. I lay down on the couch, covering myself with a spare blanket from the closet, and looked up at the ceiling of my apartment. My father's calm face held its detail in my mind. In the dream his face never changed. There was no warning of what he did to me. Or maybe I was too young to recognize the signs.

What if our DNA carried the knowledge and lessons of our parents? What if we inherited through our genes everything our parents ever learned up to the point of our conception? As babies, we wouldn't just start all over at the beginning. We would already know everything our parents knew, as well as everything they inherited from their parents, and so on and so on. In just a few generations we would have traveled further in the universe of information and advancement than millions of years in the regular world. Instead of just making the same mistakes over and over, the same mistakes our fathers made, and their fathers made before them, we could constantly be a step ahead of stupid decisions, using the memory of lessons learned before we were ever born.

I must have fallen asleep on the couch. I woke to the sounds of pots and pans in the kitchen. I heard the crack of an egg, and then the sizzle of bacon. It was six-thirty. The court hearing on the Caine motions was set for nine.

Kelly stood at the refrigerator, door open, in nothing

but a shirt and panties. She noticed I was awake.

"Good morning," she said.

"Good morning." I sat up on the couch.

"You want some breakfast?"

"No thanks, but you help yourself."

For a second, I barely recognized Kelly. When we see people our whole lives, we stop looking at their faces. We stop seeing the way they must look to strangers. She looked tired.

"Put on some clothes, Kelly. Please."

She left the bacon on the stove and went back to the bedroom. She came out wearing the blue jeans I had seen on the floor.

"What time did you come in last night?"

"I don't remember."

"Kelly, I don't mind you comin' here. I want you to have a place to go. But I need to know beforehand. That way I can wait up for you, or sleep out here on the couch so you can have the bed."

She didn't say anything. The bacon was burning. I could smell it.

"Check your bacon. It's burning."

She ate standing up in the kitchen.

"Do you have court today?"

"I do. Judge Stevens. Nine o'clock."

"Can I go with you?"

I tried not to hesitate, but it was there, between my words.

"O.K.," I answered.

"What kind of case do you have?"

"The pretrial motions on the Brad Caine case."

"Isn't that the guy charged with killing Haddie Charles?"

"That's the one."

I rubbed my eyes.

Kelly said, "If you don't want me to go, I won't."

This time I didn't hesitate. "No, it'll be fine. It might be boring, but you're welcome to come."

Kelly smiled. It was nice to see, even if she looked tired.

I took my shower and then dressed while Kelly took a shower. I heard her throw up in the shower, the sound of the heaves through the drone of the water. It wasn't the first time. She put on the same clothes but changed her hair to a ponytail. We drove together to the courthouse. I wondered if people might recognize her. She was no stranger to the courtrooms of Baldwin County. Public intoxication charges, marijuana, mostly misdemeanors. No one ever asked me about her, which was a sure sign they all knew Kelly was my daughter. Who the hell knew what they knew? What difference did it make?

We walked together through the halls of the courthouse and arrived at the courtroom of Judge Stevens. He was the first black judge in the history of Baldwin County, but more important, he was fair. Conservative, but fair. I liked the way he ran a courtroom.

Kelly sat near the back. The press hovered around waiting to get a look at the murderer in handcuffs and leg chains. They salivated at the possibility of getting a photograph or a still shot of Brad Caine smiling. Most of the reporters didn't understand the pending motions and didn't give a damn. But a picture of a smiling murderer, now that's a story.

"Good morning, Deborah."

"Good morning, Mr. Skinner."

Brad was brought in from the holding cell in the back. There must have been ten guards positioned around the room like Brad was the devil himself and might turn into smoke and escape through a rat hole. The courtroom was half-full of members of the Haddie Charles family, other lawyers, the press, and of course, Kelly. She seemed small and out of place sitting behind us. Brad saw me smile at her and asked, "Who is that?"

"Nobody. Are you ready to be on television?"

"Not really."

"Don't smile, and for God's sake, don't say anything. Every juror in this county will think they know you."

Testimony was given concerning the burglaries in Birmingham. I used the opportunity to learn all that I could learn and to cross-examine witnesses we would see again in the trial. I put on a little show for the reporters, knowing from experience they would get bored with the actual legal wranglings and leave one by one as the hearing continued.

We argued. I walked the line between laying the foundation for an appeal and giving away all my best arguments. Deborah was smart, and her boss, the district attorney of the county, was smart enough to know Deborah Webb was a better courtroom attorney than he would ever be. She did most of the talking.

Brad paid attention. He kept notes and asked me a few questions through the proceedings. As the crowd in the courtroom thinned out, I noticed Brad sneak a peek behind him. I didn't turn to look, but I knew Kelly was still there. At the end of the hearing Judge Stevens told us he would issue rulings in the next several days. He would keep his promise. Brad and I whispered a few minutes at the table before he was taken back to the jail. The trial was scheduled quickly, as we requested, and I waited in the courtroom until everyone had left. Kelly moved up to the front row as I gathered all the papers spread on the table and organized them for my file.

"He doesn't look like a murderer," Kelly said.

"They never do," I answered.

"Do you think he'll get convicted?"

"I don't know, Kelly. It's a close one. If the jury hears about those burglaries in Birmingham, they won't like it. And if they believe he lied to the police, they'll figure he's got something to hide. The gloves are a problem."

She watched me shuffle papers.

"You did a good job, Daddy. I'm glad I came to watch."

"I'm glad, too."

On the way walking out of the courtroom together Kelly said, "He's lucky to have you for a lawyer."

We drove home mostly in silence. I couldn't stop thinking about the dream. My father was always a gentle man, distant and productive. Why would I dream that he hit me?

CHAPTER 18

I have had clients through the years who called me collect from jail every day. Brad Caine never called, but he didn't have to. I visited him more often than usual.

"Brad, we need to gear up for trial. It's only a few months away, and we need to send out subpoenas. Judge Stevens has decided to allow the evidence of your Birmingham burglaries. It may end up being good grounds for an appeal. The judge also denied our motions to suppress statements and evidence."

Brad kept a box full of papers and files in his cell. He had yellow legal pads of notes and copies of cases from legal books, but unlike so many of my prior jailbird clients, Brad never tried to tell me how to do my job. He listened, asked questions, took notes, researched, but seemed immune to the jailhouse lawyer disease.

"What kind of jury do you think we want?" he asked.

"I've been thinking about that. We sure as hell don't want any old women. This is their nightmare. Living alone. The lady is killed in her own house. Left on the living room floor, bloody. Her hair messed up."

I thought about it a moment. "I think we need to get

a few of those paranoid quirky jurors looking for a conspiracy. Trying to solve the case themselves. Wondering
why Edward Polston isn't here. Looking for fingerprints,
smoking guns, secrets. Maybe lean toward minorities,
black jurors, Hispanic. They know what it's like to get
accused of something they haven't done."

I was thinking out loud and Brad drew some type of
chart as I spoke.

"What about old men?" he asked.

"Younger people would be better across the board.
The older people are gonna get hung up on the evidence
about your past burglaries."

"So," Brad said, "we want a jury of young black
Mexicans."

We both smiled. I'm not sure I could keep hold of my
sense of humor sitting in the Baldwin County Jail facing
a death sentence, but I suppose it's like everything else.
We just survive. We draw from places within ourselves,
places we may have never visited before, just to keep
going. After all, there are really only two major choices
in this life. Keep breathing or die. Take the next moment
as it comes, or not. And if we choose not to die, when the
choice is still ours to make, then we might as well smile.

"Can you think of any other witnesses besides the
guy you had lunch with in Birmingham before you came
down?" I asked.

"Phillip Ray."

"Yeah. I'm sure they'll subpoena the guy you sold the
jewelry to, and the motel clerk."

I had an idea. "I think I'll request a subpoena for
Edward Polston. That way I can wave the subpoena

around in front of the jury and talk about how the State, with all its resources and investigators, has conveniently been unable to find Mr. Polston."

"What about Junior Miflin?"

"I'll just keep Junior on call. He'll show up when we need him."

None of Brad's family members had come to our court hearing. He'd never mentioned anyone. I suggested, "If you've got any brothers and sisters, family members, it would be good to have them at the trial. We'll need them to testify at the sentencing phase if you're found guilty."

"It's just me, Mr. Skinner."

"Have you ever been married?"

"Once. A long time ago."

"Do you have any children?"

"No."

I got discouraged. "Help me out here, Brad. I'm trying to humanize you to this jury. They need to give a shit about Brad Caine. They need to be able to relate to you as a brother, or father, or something."

Brad leaned back in his chair. "Well, my parents were killed in a car accident when I was a kid. Six years old. I was in the car with them. I haven't seen my sister in ten years. She lives in Canada. I don't have any children, and I never will. I can't."

His voice asked for no sympathy. He didn't seem to know the sadness of the words. He told about himself like he was reading from a card.

"Tell me about your work, Brad. What do you do for a living?"

"I've been working as a salesman associated with a business called Products, Inc. We sell different things like fancy clocks, desk lamps, or paperweights. Shit like that. I was actually gettin' good at it. Had some regular customers."

"Will they testify?"

"Maybe. I'll make you a list. They're in Birmingham. My boss, Mr. Sherman, would be a good witness."

In every case, I have a theory. A defense theory. Juries seem to cling to giant overhanging theories. They like to take the facts, or lack of facts, and plug them into a bigger idea, a theme.

"Our theory in this case has got to be the police jumping the gun. They were under a great deal of pressure. Haddie Charles, a well-to-do older woman in a coastal town, murdered in her beach home during tourist season.

"They had to make an arrest, and they had to do it fast. You fell right into their laps out of the sky. The FBI calls and says, 'Hey, we've got this guy selling stolen jewelry to one of our snitches.' They assumed that because you ended up with the necklace, you murdered this woman. And that was it. They stopped looking for the real murderer. They stopped the investigation and became hell-bent to put together a case against you. It's the easy way out for them, but the man who killed Haddie Charles is still out there, maybe right now casing another older woman's home, laughing at the cops.

"There are no fingerprints, no physical evidence, no witnesses who can even put you positively in the area. You've paid your dues for the mistakes you made before in Birmingham. Now it's time for the investigators to find Edward Polston. It's time for them to do their jobs."

I noticed the volume of my voice rising steadily, along with my blood. There was silence at the end of the last sentence.

Brad said, "That was good. That's damn good. I like that."

"I'm glad you like it. I hope you can say you like it when this whole thing is over."

"Me too."

"Let's talk again about how to testify if you get on the witness stand. Deborah Webb is good. She won't come at you straight ahead. She'll dig a little, find a weakness, and like the flick of a switch, she'll be in your face. And then she'll back off again.

"Don't lose your patience. Say yes ma'am and no ma'am. And don't be a smartass. Nobody likes a smart-ass. Nobody. If you smile too much, or laugh, she'll eat you alive. You won't even know what you did wrong. If you try to outsmart the attorney, or ask questions back, you'll lose eventually. You have to remember you're at an extreme disadvantage on the witness stand. She gets to ask the questions, and you have to answer. You're under oath, she's not. Your life is on the line, hers isn't.

"You have to be consistent, but not repetitive. Your answers can't seem rehearsed or canned. During our entire lives our instincts as human beings continue to develop. Twelve different people, from different backgrounds, will be listening to every word you say, watching every facial expression, looking for signs you're lying, signs they don't even know they're looking for.

Using their instincts.

"Is he hiding something? Did he leave something out of his story? Why won't he look her in the eye? Why does he keep rubbing his face?"

Brad asked, "Should I look at the jury?"

"You can, but don't turn toward them after each question and deliver your answer. It looks fake. It's not normal to be asked a question by one person and then give your answer to another. But don't hesitate from time to time to look toward the jury and make eye contact with people. Don't stare anybody down, but look them square in the eye. It's harder to disbelieve a man who will look you square in the eye."

"How will I dress?"

"Rose will get you some clothes. Shirt and tie. Not overdressed or too formal. But not underdressed, disrespectful. Call her and let her know your sizes."

"How do I keep from being so nervous?"

"You should be nervous. It would be unnatural not to be nervous on a witness stand, in a crowded courtroom, in a murder trial. During my direct examination you'll settle down, have a chance to get more comfortable before the cross-examination. But during the cross-examination, you're mostly on your own. There's not a lot I can do to help you except object, break her momentum, give you small chances to collect your thoughts."

Brad continued throughout our conversation to write notes.

"Brad, later we'll go over the questions to expect. Just try to keep in mind the things I told you. The entire case could hinge on your testimony. Everything. Especially in this type of circumstantial situation."

Before I left Brad said seriously, "I'll do a good job. You'll be proud of me."

He was sincere. My mind flashed forward to that moment I knew we would have. Standing together, the jury filing into the courtroom to take their seats after hours of deliberation, the foreperson holding a folded piece of paper with the verdict.

Lightheaded, watching the faces of the jurors one by one to see if they look at me. When a jury is about to deliver a guilty verdict they won't look at the defendant or his lawyer. They won't even glance in that direction.

And then the bailiff takes the piece of paper from the foreperson, walks over and hands it to the judge. The judge takes a moment to read it to himself, and then, surrounded by silence, the verdict is delivered in just a few words. There is immediate shock or exhilaration. And just as immediately, relief for the lawyer. Either way. If it's not guilty, the relief is in the victory. If it's guilty, the relief is in the knowledge that the lawyer will live to fight another day, another fight, while the defendant is taken away in handcuffs.

God, what a moment.

CHAPTER 19

Rose came in and sat down in my office. It was unusual. In fact, I can't remember two or three times she ever came in and just sat down across the desk from me.

"What's the matter, Rose?"

"There's lots the matter. I just wonder sometimes if you notice."

"You mean the bills?" I asked.

"For one thing, the bills, yes. They're not getting paid. There's no money to pay them with. And I can't even pay my own bills at home. Cindy's sick. She can't work. I've been with you thirty years, but I can't live like this. You spent all the five thousand dollars from Brad Caine toward back taxes and other bills. I understand, but I still can't live like this."

I was trying to remember who the hell Cindy was.

Rose was on a roll. "You just sit in here shuffling papers, waiting until three o'clock to have your first drink. The only case you ever work on is Brad Caine."

I looked closely at her face. It was how I always remembered it to be. Had she been young once? Had she always worn glasses?

"You look like hell, Jack. Look at yourself. You don't eat right. You don't exercise. You let people like Becky speak to you like you don't care anymore. Maybe it's none of my business. Maybe I should just keep my nose out of it. But who else is gonna tell you? Nobody."

I could see it was difficult for her. Rose had probably thought about this conversation for weeks, maybe even months, before she came in and sat down across from me. She deserved something.

I said, "We're just having a down time, Rose. It'll pick up. Maybe you're right. Maybe my mind is too occupied with the Caine case. There's just something about it I can't quite put my finger on.

"Most of the cases I've handled through the years, I couldn't remember anything about them if you sat the file in my lap. Thousands. But some cases, just a few, I can't forget.

"Remember the Gabriel Black case? Years ago. I was young, still taking appointed cases. It was a capital murder. I still think about it. I don't know why. He was probably guilty. But there was something about it I just couldn't explain then, and I still can't explain it now. Just a feeling. For lack of a better word, it haunts me.

"This Brad Caine case is the same way. Different, but the same. I can't get my mind around the problem. Maybe I'm just gettin' old, Rose. Maybe it's time I found something else to do."

Her face gave no clue about how she felt. We just sat in the room a moment, the phone noticeably quiet.

"Don't give up yet, Rose. The trial isn't far away. Everything will be back to normal when it's over."

It was a bad excuse. I knew it was a bad excuse, but it was the only one I could think of. Things had started going wrong long before Brad Caine ever came to my office. I just didn't want Rose to leave. She was one of the few constants in my life. She was dependable in a world I couldn't depend upon. If I had a hundred-dollar bill in my wallet, I would have handed it to her.

Rose stood and walked from my office. I listened to her sounds in the other room, trying to get a fix on whether she was packing to leave, or sitting down to stay. The phone rang. Thank God. We both knew what it meant. If she answered the phone, she was staying. If she let it ring, I was on my own.

After the first ring, there was a second. The time between the rings seemed unusually long. And then came the third ring. I closed my eyes.

I heard Rose say, "Jack Skinner, attorney at law."

I was saved. The clock said 3:05. I decided to hold off until after five o'clock to visit Mr. Whiskey. It was the proper thing to do.

Rose said good-bye at her usual time and left for home. I watched out my window until her car turned the corner before I fixed myself a glass. I hadn't heard from Kelly in almost two weeks. No calls, no surprise visits. It was the usual pattern.

The phone rang. It was Deborah Webb.

"Jack Skinner. Are you answering your own phones now?"

"I'm working late."

"Putting in extra time on the Haddie Charles case?"

"It's the Brad Caine case, not the Haddie Charles case. And no, I'm ready right now. How 'bout yourself?"

"I'll be ready," she said.

"What can I do for you, Ms. Webb?"

"I want to talk to you about your letter they found by the body. You got a copy in the discovery packet. I don't see any reason to make it an issue in the trial, unless you do. I just wanted you to know up front I wouldn't be trying to sneak it in the back door."

"I don't think it's relevant."

"I agree," she said.

If it had been another prosecutor, I would have questioned the motive of the phone call, but Deborah was just being straight. She was right, it wasn't relevant. But if it got in front of the jury, it could cause a problem. The jury wouldn't like the fact I'd represented the dead woman before, tried to squeeze her for money, and now I was representing her accused murderer. It wouldn't sit well.

"Is that all?" I asked.

"That's all. Did you ask your boy about a possible plea?"

"I did. He's not interested. It's hard to convince an innocent man he should plead guilty to something he didn't do and spend the rest of his life in the penitentiary. You know?"

Deborah said, "He's guilty, Jack. We can do it the easy way, or we can do it the hard way. You remember Gabriel Black?"

It struck me. Out of all the cases, all the trials we'd had, why would she be thinking of the same name, the same case? My delay in answering was noticeable.

The words folded out. "I guess we'll do it the hard way."

We hung up.

I sat a long time in thought before I drove to Buddy's for a greasy cheeseburger. After Rose's speech, I should've had a salad, but a salad just wouldn't do. No, a salad wouldn't do.

When I walked in the door of Buddy's the first person I saw was Kelly sitting in the corner. She was with a strange man, both smoking cigarettes, when her eyes caught mine. I walked directly to her table and sat down. Through the years of constant confrontations in the courtroom, my fear of confrontations in the real world had virtually disappeared.

The man had a beard and wore a black leather jacket. His teeth were the color of clay and there was hair on the backs of his hands.

"Hey, Daddy," Kelly said.

I gestured toward the man. "Who's your friend?"

She reacted like a little girl caught with a half-eaten cookie.

"Wayne. Wayne," she said twice.

"Do you mind if I talk to my daughter alone, Wayne?"

He waited a moment too long. A challenge in the world of men. And then he stood, pushing his chair back loudly, and walked toward the pool table.

I asked Kelly, "Where you been stayin'?"

"Different places. Don't be so mean."

"Why do you go to people like Wayne? Why? I don't understand. You're pretty. You're smart. And you sit in the corners of dirty bars with men like Wayne. Explain it to me."

"I can't explain it. He bought me a drink."

I was in a shitty mood. First Rose, then Deborah's comment about Gabriel Black, and now Kelly. A trifecta of women in some unspoken conspiracy to piss me off. I felt like actually getting in a fight, win or lose, just for the fuck of it.

Instead, I asked, "Are you hungry?"

"Yes."

"Do you want a cheeseburger?"

"O.K."

"Or would you rather have a salad?"

"No."

"Good," I said.

Lola brought us two cheeseburgers. Wayne hovered nearby, obviously waiting for me to leave so Kelly could be his again.

"Do you have a job?" I asked.

"No." She picked at her cheeseburger.

"I wish I could put you to work at the office," I said, without putting much thought into the suggestion.

"That would be nice," she said quickly with a smile. "I'd like that."

I felt guilty backing out of the offer. "I don't know what you could do."

"Maybe I could help you with your cases. Help you get everything organized for court. When is the trial for Brad Caine?"

I ordered another drink and had Lola bring Kelly a Coke.

"It's not far away, but I don't know what you could do," I said again.

She was excited. "I could be like an assistant. You don't have to pay me. We could do it for room and board. It could be like my share of the rent. I could move in for a while."

It would keep her off the street, I thought. Then I remembered Becky.

"Your sister wouldn't like that."

Kelly said with some authority, "Who cares? She's not my keeper. I'll stay where I want."

Kelly had a smile. She seemed happy, if only for a moment. It was more than I could resist.

"O.K.," I said, "but I've got conditions. No drinking. No drugs. And no Wayne, or anybody else like him. You be home by a reasonable hour. And no cartoons. I hate that damn roadrunner. He pisses me off."

We both laughed. Kelly took a sip from her Coke, and we walked past Big Wayne on our way out the door. I gave him a look. In the world of men, we both knew what it meant.

CHAPTER 20

Kelly moved into my home. It had been a long time since I had lived with a woman. I had forgotten what they can do to a bathroom. I slept the first night on the couch and the next day we rode together to meet with Junior Miflin before going to see Brad Caine.

Junior was sitting in the same booth at the Waffle House. Kelly and I sat down across from the man. With his head bent down low near the top of a cup of coffee, Junior's eyes stayed on Kelly. I introduced them.

"Mornin'," Junior Miflin said.

"Mornin'," Kelly answered. She picked up and put down the menu several times before she ordered just a cup of coffee.

"Any luck findin' Edward Polston?" I asked.

"No. He ain't nowhere. Disappeared. Best thing I got was the information about workin' offshore in Texas or Louisiana. I got the investigator at the D.A.'s office to admit they can't find him neither."

Kelly's cup of coffee arrived. Junior and I watched as she turned up the sugar jar and kept pouring. She filled it with cream until the tan liquid threatened to sneak over the top. I remembered watching a street person mix such a cup of coffee one time in New Orleans. It looked thick like syrup. Junior couldn't seem to pull his eyes away from Kelly more than a few seconds in a row.

Junior said, "I've got an old buddy in the Department of Motor Vehicles up in Montgomery. He's gettin' a printout of every car, the same make and model as Caine's, with the same first digits in the tag, same color, registered in the state. But here's your problem. You know the first few numbers and letters designate the county of registration? Caine's car was registered in Birmingham, Jefferson County. So how many of those cars on the printout, same make and model and color with Birmingham plates, were all the way down here in Baldwin County on the day of the murder? You see what I mean?"

"I see what you mean, but I don't have to prove how many of those cars were in Gulf Shores. I can just slam my fist down on the printout and make the prosecutor prove it wasn't one of those other cars driving around the neighborhood of Haddie Charles."

Kelly listened. She pretended not to notice Junior's stare, but it was starting to piss me off.

In a low tone I asked, "You want me to wrap her up in a doggie bag to take home?"

The question, and the tone, seemed to catch Junior off guard.

"Sorry," he mumbled.

Changing the subject I asked, "Got anything else, Junior?"

He turned back to me and said, "Your boy's keepin'

his nose clean in jail. Keepin' his mouth shut. You need me for the trial, or just stay on call?"

"I'll let you know a few days before."

When I moved to slide from the booth, Kelly drank down the rest of her coffee and held the cup upright a few seconds too long for every single brown drop. It made me remember again the homeless man in New Orleans who had done the same thing like there were sprinkles of gold dust in the bottom of the mug that he just couldn't leave behind.

Kelly and I walked to the front door of the Baldwin County Jail, and I rang the buzzer. She was still very nervous, wringing her hands together and looking back and forth. I handed Kelly the file to occupy her arms and also to make her look like an actual assistant.

We sat down in the meeting room on the safe side of the screen and waited for Brad Caine.

"It's cold in here," Kelly said quietly. We both knew she'd spent more than her share of nights shivering in the dark on a cool cement floor. The image made me rub my face. Kelly jumped when the steel door popped open and Brad Caine entered.

"Hi," Brad said.

"Brad, this is my daughter, Kelly. She's helping me with your case, keeping everything organized. Kelly, this is Brad Caine."

Brad nodded his head in Kelly's direction and then started pulling papers out of his box while Kelly seemed unable to remove her eyes from the man on the other side of the screen, until she noticed me notice, and then looked down and began taking notes.

"Junior hasn't been able to find Edward Polston, and apparently neither has anyone else."

"Is that good or bad?" Brad asked.

"Well, like I said before, probably good. It leaves a hole in their case. I'd hate for Polston to show up and have some alibi to challenge your story of meeting with him that morning and getting the necklace."

"Anything on the car tag?" Brad asked.

"Yeah. Junior's got a printout of cars, same color, same make, same model, same Jefferson County registration. It'll play good in the courtroom."

Kelly was writing furiously. Brad Caine looked her way and remarked with a smile, "Like father, like daughter."

I don't know if he was commenting on our tireless note-taking or on the fact we were both left-handed. Kelly looked up and then back down quickly like a little girl who hasn't yet learned how to hide her feelings. Brad seemed unconcerned.

"I think we're all ready for trial, Brad. I can't think of anything that'll keep us from going on Judge Stevens's next trial docket. I want to talk to you one more time about your testimony."

Brad riffled through the pages of his yellow legal pad until he located the page titled "*Testimony*."

I waited until he was ready.

"Listen closely, please. It's hard to explain, Brad, but there's an air of believability that can almost never be faked. It's a believability that comes with the truth, or at least a person's deep-rooted belief in what they're saying. There's not a formula or script to follow. It's a delicate combination of the words a person speaks, and the manner in which those words are delivered to the listeners.

"I've seen witnesses speak utter bullshit but do it in a believable way. It's rare. I've seen witnesses speak the complete and total unequivocal truth but look like children caught in pitiful lies.

"I can do my job better than it's ever been done, and you can get convicted on your own testimony. Or on the other hand, I can beat around like a drunk man in a refrigerator box the whole trial, and you can set yourself free with your own words. It is a power never to be underestimated. The air of believability. The power of perception. One man's perception of another, based on what can be seen, or heard, or felt in the bones. There's no substitute, no comparison. God gave us instincts to protect and preserve, and these instincts allow us to gauge and calculate our fellow men as trustworthy or liars. As someone to depend upon, or as someone who will crush the skull of an old lady for a handful of diamonds and gold."

About halfway through my speech I noticed Kelly staring past me at Brad Caine. Brad never moved his eyes from mine, holding the gaze until I'd finished, conquering any desire he may have had to glance at my daughter who sat beside me with a file in her lap.

The meeting was over.

CHAPTER 21

My life fell into a peculiar routine. Kelly washed my clothes, ironed my shirts, and the apartment smelled of supper each night when I came through the door. I'd seen it before, Kelly on the upswing. Clean and full of potential with neat little promises wrapped in pretty paper. But I'd never seen her take to a home situation with such force and comfort.

I slept on the couch. Each night we would stay up, watch T.V., read the paper, talk about the Caine case. She was still a beautiful girl, her hair pulled back into a ponytail, a piece always hanging down alongside her face and curling near the edge of her mouth. She seemed to have nothing of me in her. At least I couldn't see it. God help me, there were times I wondered if she was mine. But her mother was a pious woman, unaffected by lust, or vanity, or any of the other seven deadly sins. Some of my finest negotiations came in her bedroom. They weren't always successful, but they were damn clever if I do say so myself.

Kelly was sitting in her place on the couch watching cartoons on T.V. I was in the chair, Echo in my lap, the newspaper folded sideways to read next to my leg. She said, "Do you want to be cremated?"

"Right now?" I asked.

Kelly faked a little laugh and said, "I'm serious. I don't even know. Do you want to be cremated? Do you believe in staying on those life support machines?"

She was serious.

"I don't care what you do with me as long as you promise not to put me in one of those rest homes," I said.

Kelly had a puzzled look on her face, like she hadn't considered such a thing.

"You don't remember when you were a kid visiting your Grandpa Weber, your momma's father, at that place on the coast? How crazy he acted toward the end, with that ridiculous safari hat?"

Her face was blank. There were pieces missing. Drugs and alcohol and self-pity had punched holes in her memory. I caught my eyes drifting to the place where Kelly's oversized white T-shirt stopped on her thigh. It shouldn't have been a fight. It shouldn't have been a temptation. I looked away, down at the newspaper, and considered the possibility that the temptation was a sign Kelly wasn't mine. Surely God and nature would know the difference.

I heard myself say, "Don't you want any babies?"

Kelly's head tilted a bit to the side like a dog hearing a new sound. The piece of hair hanging along the side of her face eased over and caught the wetness of her lip. For a moment I actually thought she had drifted into a catatonic state.

"I'm too old to have babies."

"Not yet, but you will be if you don't hurry up."

Kelly asked, "Why is it women only have a window of time to have babies, but men can make babies until they're a hundred years old?"

I was half-listening and half-reading a story about a woman who killed her husband with a baseball bat while he slept and then left his body in the closet for five days until she couldn't stand the smell.

"Well, I think the answer to that question is that God intended women to take care of their children. They need to be strong physically, within a certain healthy age category. Not just strong physically to deliver the child, but also strong to protect the child, and provide.

"Maybe God never intended the man to do anything except spread the seed. That's why it doesn't matter if he's eighteen or eighty-eight. That's why it doesn't matter if he's physically capable of providing for, protecting, or even holding a baby."

I never looked up as I spoke. A few moments passed before Kelly asked, "Do you really believe that?"

I didn't answer. The woman in the story told her friends the husband had run off with the rodeo. She didn't have any visible scratches or bruises. There was blood across the headboard like she had waited for him to drift to sleep, the back of his head must have been teed up nicely on the pillow, and with a full swing of the bat she crushed his skull like a pomegranate. What a way to go.

"Do you want some vanilla ice cream?" Kelly asked.

I turned from the paper to look at her. When I was a

child my grandfather used to sit in his big brown leather chair and eat a bowl of vanilla ice cream every night after dinner. It was a ritual centered around the simple enjoyment of a bowl of ice cream, and it continued until the night he died.

"O.K.," I answered.

Echo's eyes followed Kelly as she passed our chair on her way to the kitchen. Yosemite Sam was on the television, pissed off and hostile. What a strange role model for our children. "Mom, I want to be just like Yosemite Sam when I grow up." If just one child in the universe said such a thing, the demented little cowboy would be a proven instrument of the devil.

Kelly came back and handed me a white bowl with a few scoops of vanilla ice cream. The bowl was cool, and Echo watched me take a bite, probably wishing she could find something like ice cream during her rat-hunting expeditions.

"What is that Yosemite Sam guy mad about?" I asked.

Kelly spoke about him like he was a real person. "I'm not sure, but you're right, he does seem to be angry most of the time. He shouldn't carry guns."

We watched Sam shoot the side of a barn two hundred times in a few seconds.

"Kelly?"

"Yes."

"He's not real."

"Who's not real?"

"Yosemite Sam. He's not real."

Kelly smiled. "I know that, Daddy."

We watched as the cartoon character stomped around in his oversized boots talking about the barn he just shot.

Kelly asked, "Has Brad Caine ever been married?"

I finished my bowl of delicious ice cream. My grandfather was no fool. He died at home, thirty minutes after his last bowl of the good stuff, unlike Grandpa Weber, alone in a strange rest home, probably feeling abandoned by his family, cast aside as life flew down the highway around him.

"Why'd you ask that?"

"Just curious," Kelly said.

"I think he was married once, a long time ago. He said he didn't have any kids. His parents died when he was young."

Kelly watched me as I spoke and then asked, "Are you nervous about the trial?"

"Not really," I answered. My gut churned at the thought of standing up from my chair in the crowded courtroom and turning to the jury. An old lawyer once told me, "When you're not nervous anymore, when you don't feel the fire in your belly before the opening bell, you need to find something else to do."

"I don't think he's guilty," Kelly said. "I just don't think he's guilty," she repeated to herself, turning back to the cartoon.

I set the bowl down on the floor for the cat. Echo sniffed suspiciously and licked the thick cream. As her tongue darted in and out delivering the taste, the cat's eyes looked around for the hand she expected to steal away her treat any second. I watched her lick the bowl clean.

We sat in silence in the room for thirty minutes, the volume of the television low, me reading the paper. Finally Kelly said, "I don't remember Grandpa Weber acting crazy. I just remember him being happy."

I thought about it. Maybe she was right.

CHAPTER 22

It was the night before trial. On the kitchen table I had papers spread out. I was making notes and putting together a timeline. Kelly was back and forth from the kitchen to me, filling my glass, cooking dinner, watching some silly television show out of the corners of her blue eyes.

I was jotting down jury questions when there was a pounding on the door that shook the apartment. Kelly's head swung from the T.V. to the door, and I started to stand. The door flew open, slamming against the wall. Becky entered in a rage. Covered up in anger. I had never seen her with such pointed vengeance. If she had been holding a gun I'd have expected the trigger to be pulled without a word, an explosion, and blood. My own blood, seeping from my belly, traveling slowly into my pants and pooling below my feet, dark red.

In a remarkably calm voice she said, "Have you just set up house? Moved Kelly in? Like a wife? She cooks and cleans for you? Shares your bed? Like the couple next door? Perfectly normal?"

Equally composed, but with a sharp edge, I said, "Shut your mouth."

I noticed the cat slink in the door and sit at Becky's feet, deceived by the calmness of the conversation. Becky turned to Kelly where she stood near the kitchen counter. "It's sick, Kelly. It's sick."

And then there was silence. It appeared Kelly had something to say. We waited. The expectation was enormous.

In a low voice Kelly said, "I'm pregnant."

And there was silence again. I looked at her stomach, covered with the typical oversized T-shirt. I wondered how I hadn't noticed before, hadn't suspected. The sounds of her throwing up in the bathroom. The loose-fitting clothes.

For a moment, just a moment, it seemed perhaps we would come together. Rally around the crisis. Rejoice at the idea of a new life. Hope. But the moment passed, and Becky turned to face me where I sat at the far end of the table, papers spread before me.

Becky charged like a bull, her stout body shooting forward in a collection of fury and inertia. She was on me before I could stand, her full weight upon me, hands around my throat, and we fell like large animals onto the floor. It was beyond comprehension. I landed on my back, caught without a breath in my lungs.

I felt the blast of a punch against the side of my head, and a knee like fire in my crotch, sending my oxygen into space. Out of the side of my eye I saw Echo still sitting by the door, wide-eyed and transfixed. A far cry from the sweet taste of vanilla ice cream on the bottom of a bowl. I remember specifically thinking, this must be how it feels to be mauled by a bear. A bottom-

less irrational pit of violence. A hurricane of pain and
adrenaline.

I managed to twist Becky off the top of me. We were
on the carpet, front to front, as I tried to get hold of her
wrists, to slow down the claws gouging my face. Her
mouth was contorted, one side pulled down in a ridiculous frown.

I felt Kelly between us, wedging her body between
her sister and her father as we fought on the floor. She
was screaming, "Stop! Stop! Stop!" over and over, until
Becky abruptly stopped moving, Kelly's arms wrapped
around her. The silence returned. I could hear the rain
outside.

Kelly finally said, "You're crazy, Becky. He didn't do
anything."

When I heard Kelly's words, it was the first time I
realized why Becky had done what she'd done. She
believed I was the father of the child. The child of my
own child. She believed it completely. I felt a trickle of
blood roll from my nose. From where I lay, Kelly's head
blocked my vision of Becky's face.

I heard Becky say, "Then who's the father, Kelly?
Who is it?"

Kelly answered quickly, and with a strength in her
voice. "I don't know who it is. It doesn't matter. But it
isn't Daddy. He's just giving me a place to live. A safe
place while I'm pregnant."

The two women's faces must have been only inches
apart. Like a man in the woods waiting for the bear to go
away, I just stayed still and listened.

"I don't believe you, Kelly. I know what I know.

Don't come see me again. Don't ask for my help. You've made your choice, and you're on your own. He'll turn his back on you when you need him the most, like he's always done. But I won't be there for you next time. I won't."

Over Kelly's shoulder I saw Becky lift herself to a sitting position. Her hair was all over the place, and she was bleeding slightly from the edge of her mouth. Becky's eyes had changed. I knew she had reached the crossroads. I knew I might never see her again, or if I did, it would be from a distance.

As Becky looked down at me, my head resting on the carpet, she began to pat her hair into place, watching me as she pulled it back behind each ear and then dabbed the blood from her lip with her white fingers. She stood, straightening her shirt, and took a very deep breath with her eyes closed. A few seconds later Becky's eyes opened again and she looked down at me and Kelly on the floor, stretched out next to each other, a few stray papers scattered around. There was no expression on her face. None at all. She simply stepped over us and walked from the apartment leaving the door open.

The rain grew steadily louder as I listened for the sound of Becky's shoes in the breezeway and her car door closing. A brief thought entered my mind that maybe she was getting a gun from the car and would be back to end the misery. But then the car started and the sound of the engine slowly moved away until it was gone.

Kelly stood and collected the papers on the floor. I watched as she placed them in a neat stack on the table. I tried to imagine a baby inside her. It was hard to do.

"How far along are you?" I asked.

"Five and a half, six months. Something like that."

I sat up and leaned my back against the wall for support. The blood under my nose had half-dried, smearing when I wiped it with my shirt. The cat watched me with curiosity, never having seen me on the floor, eye level.

On the way to the kitchen Kelly said, "We're having casserole tonight for supper."

Her mother used to make casserole. I hated it. I hated the thought of it. Casserole. I would stare down at the plate and feel my stomach tighten. I would watch the children eating around the table and want to slap their faces for not knowing the difference.

CHAPTER 23

I didn't sleep worth a damn all night. I drove with Kelly to the courthouse harboring thoughts of causes to delay the trial. Maybe there was a mix-up and nobody received a jury summons. Maybe a hurricane had formed overnight in the Gulf and the judge would cancel court. But when we arrived, the sky was clear and the lack of parking spots left no doubt that people had arrived for jury duty.

I looked forward to the first punch. It would take away the butterflies, take away the doubts. I could dig in, attack, and then dig in again. The underdog with a cause.

Rose had rounded up clothes for Brad Caine. He sat alone at the defense table when Kelly and I entered the courtroom. There were three deputies positioned inside the room and a fourth at the front door. The jury would certainly receive the message that Brad Caine was a dangerous man, despite his pleasant appearance at the table.

The jury selection in a capital murder case is long and tedious. Panels of jurors, ten or twelve people at a time, are brought in the courtroom to endure questions from the attorneys and the judge. The obvious purpose is to find twelve men and women who can listen to the evidence and return a fair and impartial verdict. Reaching this goal in a capital murder case is complicated by the moral issue of capital punishment and the access of jurors to information from the media. For the months since the murder of Haddie Charles the newspapers and television news programs covered every step in the process, never failing to run the mugshot photograph of Brad above the story. A hint to future defendants: try not to look like a murderer or a smartass when you're arrested and photographed at your local jail.

The jury selection process is a good place to begin planting the seeds of a defense. I asked the prospective jurors whether or not they knew Edward Polston, the man we believed may have killed Haddie Charles and stolen her jewelry. I asked them whether they considered DNA evidence and fingerprint evidence to be reliable, and then told them no such evidence existed in the Brad Caine case. I challenged their belief in the idea that a man is innocent until proven guilty by asking if they could honestly say that Brad Caine, as he sat in the courtroom at the defense table before the trial, was considered as innocent of this crime as any man walking down the sidewalk outside the courthouse.

I recognized faces and tried to place them. I would be removing anyone related to law enforcement, or anyone whose home had been burglarized, or anyone over fifty-five, or anyone exposed to the regular media reports. Occasionally I glanced toward the door where the big black eye of a television camera stared through the window at us. Newspaper reporters came and went, slowly worn down by the monotonous routine. Family members of Haddie Charles watched me like I was a big red devil in a suit and tie.

Kelly sat on our side of the courtroom alone. It was like a wedding where the groom has no friends or family and his side remains empty while across the aisle there is barely room to find an open seat. I expected Brad to look her way, just out of curiosity. But for the entire morning, he didn't.

On the fourth panel sat a man named Larry Foley. He was the father of a boy I had represented five years earlier in juvenile court. I saved the boy's ass and his daddy was a hardworking man who didn't forget the people who helped him along the way. He managed to avoid responding to questions such as: "Has Mr. Skinner ever represented you in a legal proceeding?" and "Are you a friend or a blood relative of any of the attorneys participating in this case?"

The district attorney's office was removing people who waffled on their commitment to the death penalty, and young women who might lean toward the handsome defendant, and people who had been charged with a crime or falsely accused of a crime. Larry Foley didn't fit in any of these categories. He just looked straight ahead at whoever asked him the questions.

By the end of the afternoon we'd gone through all eight panels. The judge dismissed everyone and requested that we return for the actual selection of the jury the next morning. Brad was taken back to the jail, where Kelly and I met with him in the conference room.

I had begun to go through the list with Brad, Kelly sitting behind me, when I was called outside of the room to speak with Deborah Webb on the telephone. On my way back into the conference room I heard Kelly and Brad Caine talking. The conversation ended as I entered. The only word I clearly heard was Kelly's last. "No."

We talked about jurors we liked and jurors we didn't. I decided to keep the information about Larry Foley to myself. I'd learned from experience that after a defendant was found guilty, and languished in prison for a period of time, he often would file documents against his lawyers claiming ineffective assistance of counsel. In those documents a defendant would utilize any and all information he possessed to gain an advantage, any advantage at all.

"I don't much like number eighty-six, Larry Foley," Brad said, his finger sliding down a long list.

"Why not?" I asked.

"He looks pissed off. He didn't really answer any questions."

"Sometimes that's good," I added.

"Do you know him?" Brad asked.

"Not really, but there are a lot of other people I'd rather remove than number eighty-six."

Brad moved down the list. Kelly took notes. My mind began to drift to opening arguments that would be the true beginning of the battle. I caught a brief smell of perfume, out of place in a cold gray jail. It was from Kelly. Her hair was pulled back in a ponytail. Her legs were crossed appropriately. I remembered that a tiny baby was in there somewhere, hidden away from the world, which didn't seem like such a bad idea. I was nervous, but ready. Anxious, but prepared. And when I looked at Brad Caine, I wondered what was going through his mind. The mind of a man with his life on the line, innocent or guilty. To be killed on a random day, at a random time, at some unknown moment in our stream of life is bad enough. But to be condemned to death in a formal proceeding, leaving freedom at the door, and then having a certain day, and a certain time, marked in red on a certain calendar is inhuman. To count down the minutes like drops of water falling between the eyes of the man tied to the table. To wait your turn and then expect to find even a pinpoint of dignity in the final moment, years later. Who exactly have we killed?

CHAPTER 24

Kelly was very quiet on the ride to the courthouse the next morning. I sensed her fear for Brad Caine.

"Don't get too attached," I said.

"What do you mean?"

"In this business you've got to keep yourself separated from the clients. Whether they're guilty or not doesn't matter," I added.

I wanted to say, "Don't be stupid. Haven't you learned anything from all those assholes you dated and slept with? Haven't you learned your weakness for bad men? Men who use you, and hit you? Men who take advantage of you? Don't let it happen. Stop it before it happens this time or you might find yourself driving up to the prison twice a month to visit a man on death row. A man with a certain red mark on a certain calendar."

But I didn't say it. She'd heard it all before. Besides, my mind was on the trial, opening arguments, the first punch. My belly was in a knot, tied tight with black coffee and the absence of food. I was never able to eat during trial weeks. Food smells made me sick.

We took our positions in the courtroom. Judge

Stevens entertained several motions, including motions to remove jurors for cause, and then finally we sat down to strike the jury. Deborah would call out a number, and then I would, and then Deborah, again and again until each of us had removed the people we found most offensive. We were left theoretically with the twelve most neutral and impartial people on the panel. Larry Foley made the cut and took his place on the center front row of the jury box. He would be my focal point.

The jury was a strong mix of young and old, men and women. There were two black jurors, one girl with a lazy eye, and a fat man who could barely fit in his chair. I studied their faces, mostly the eyes. They were out of their routines. Pulled away from their children, desk jobs, farmland, to sit and determine the fate of a man named Brad Caine.

Deborah Webb stood to deliver her opening statement. The words swam around me as I jotted notes I would never read and tried to get my mind right. I heard her say, "A single blow to the right side of her head." Bits and pieces of sentences lodged in my memory.

"Six months ago to the day...killed in her own home...her skull crushed...left to bleed to death...her finger severed for the family ring...jewelry stolen, cash.

"Brad Caine's car identified in the victim's neighborhood the afternoon before the murder...videotape of the man selling a stolen necklace the next day to Curt Junkins, the same man Brad Caine went to in the past to sell his stolen goods...and the defendant says to Curt Junkins, 'There might be more'...and he lied to police, and said he wasn't even in Baldwin County until the early morning hours of the day after the murder, despite the fact his car was seen Sunday afternoon in the neighborhood."

It sounded bad, but then again, it always sounds bad after the prosecutor paints the first picture. Deborah wasn't finished.

"Burglars have patterns. Brad Caine has a pattern. Always breaks in a house the same way. Always steals jewelry. Always sells the stolen jewelry to Curt Junkins. And always, always uses gloves so no fingerprints are left. When he was arrested, hidden in the drop ceiling of his motel room, we found these rubber gloves. Freshly washed. Wet."

I watched the eyes of the jurors. They followed every word, every gesture. I turned slightly to see the newspaper and television reporters writing in their little pads. The big black eye was at the window. Kelly sat quietly. Brad Caine watched it all like it wasn't real. It wasn't really happening. Like a daydream.

Deborah Webb finished and sat down.

Judge Stevens nodded at me and said, "Mr. Skinner, opening remarks?"

I sat stone still. The effect of silence in a courtroom is overwhelming. They waited for me to rise. They waited to hear what could possibly be said. The first blow had been struck.

I stood and slowly raised my arms on each side, bent slightly at the elbow, into the air, up to shoulder level.

"You know, maybe we don't need a trial for Brad Caine. Maybe you folks could just go back to the jury room, take a vote, and convict Brad Caine of the murder of Haddie Charles. Sentence him to death by lethal injection.

"And then, five years from now, we can all read in the newspaper about the police actually finding the man who really did kill this lady. And the man confessing. But it would be too late, wouldn't it? Too late to ask the questions that should've been asked in this trial. Too late to hold the district attorney's office to their burden of proof under the law."

I stood still, slowly lowering my arms back to my sides. The eyes of the jurors asked for more. More explanations. Guidance.

"For instance, where's the murder weapon? It wasn't in Brad Caine's motel room, or on the videotape.

"Where's the rest of the stolen jewelry, or the woman's finger, or the camera, or the other things stolen from Haddie Charles? They won't tell you, because they don't know.

"And where's Edward Polston, the man who gave Brad Caine the stolen necklace to pay off a debt the morning before Brad sold it? The man we believe has the other stolen jewelry, and the camera, and the ring from Haddie Charles's finger? Where is he?

"The reason you won't hear about Brad Caine's blood, or hair, or fingerprints in the house of Haddie Charles is because he was never in the house of Haddie Charles.

"The reason you won't hear about Brad Caine having any connection to Ms. Charles, or any knowledge she had a lot of jewelry in her home, is because he had no connection. He had no knowledge. But Edward Polston did.

"The reason you won't hear evidence of witnesses seeing Brad Caine in the neighborhood, or his complete tag number on the car, is because he was never in the neighborhood. And his car was in Birmingham with him at the time of the murder."

I lowered my voice. There's nothing like a whisper. It can literally pull a juror physically toward the speaker. Larry Foley's body leaned slightly forward.

"Brad Caine is a working man. He made mistakes in the past and paid for those mistakes in full. I believe the police were in a bad spot. An elderly lady, killed in her home on the beach. It was tourist season. The pressure was on. None of us likes to think a murderer is loose among us. In the line with us at the grocery store. In the car next to us at the drive-through window at the bank. Creeping around our neighborhoods.

"So when they got the news Brad Caine had sold a piece of the stolen jewelry, they'd found their man. End of investigation. End of story. The pressure was off. Everyone could feel safe again.

"Don't believe it. Don't fall for it. It's not the end of the story. The person who murdered Haddie Charles is still out there.

"If you want to convict Brad Caine of selling stolen jewelry he didn't know was stolen, do it. If you want to convict him of being at the wrong place at the wrong time, do it. But for God's sake, don't convict the man of a murder he didn't commit and sentence him to death without asking all the questions, and demanding that the district attorney's office, and the police, and the State of Alabama answer those questions to your satisfaction."

I stood motionless again, looking across the faces of the jurors, challenging each one to look me in the eye. Not one turned away.

I walked over and sat down next to my client. Judge Stevens cut the day short to attend to some personal matters, and we all agreed to start the next morning with the State's first witness, Investigator Randy Riley.

CHAPTER 25

The courtroom cleared and only Kelly was left. She had a different look on her face.

"Daddy, that was fantastic. It was like a church sermon. I couldn't move a muscle. Those people won't convict him, not after that."

"It's just the opening arguments. They'll decide to convict him or cut him loose based on the evidence, or the lack of evidence. At least that's what they're supposed to do."

My legs were heavy as we walked to the car together. I'm always surprised by the amount of energy expended in the courtroom just sitting in a chair or standing in front of a jury. A trial attorney has to focus every second, on every word spoken, on body language, on all the tiny details. I've lost ten or twelve pounds in jury trials that lasted less than a week. I guess if I had a trial that lasted a few months I'd disappear completely.

We rode together the two blocks to the county jail and parked in front. Kelly got out of the car to go inside with me to meet with Brad Caine. I'm not sure exactly why, maybe it was Kelly's haste to exit the car, but I didn't want her in the meeting.

"You wait out here. I'll be back in a little while."

She hesitated slightly. "O.K."

The meeting didn't last long. Brad was excited.

"I need you to keep notes, Brad. People remember things better when they write them down. I want you to take notes on every witness. If you testify, you'll be asked questions that arise from the testimony of every witness. Your answers have to fit with the timelines, and the facts from every person who testifies. If you give one answer that doesn't fit, the jury will have to decide someone is lying, and you've got the most to lose. The other witnesses don't get to listen to each other. You do. Take advantage of it."

Brad asked, "How'd you think it went today?"

"It's too early to tell anything."

"I didn't like the way a few of those jurors looked after the D.A. did her opening argument. They looked like they'd already made up their minds."

"We've got a long way to go, Brad. Don't get paranoid on me yet. Concentrate on your job, testifying. This case is all circumstantial, but the jury will be looking for someone to hold responsible for this murder."

Brad Caine rubbed his eyes. I could tell he, too, was exhausted. The emotional strain was all over his face. I wanted to give him reassurance. I wanted to tell him everything would be all right. But I'd learned that lesson many years earlier in the Gabriel Black case. Never make promises to clients you can't keep. Never predict the outcome of a jury trial, twelve people, locked in a room, with no legal experience, deciding the fate of other human beings. I've talked to jurors who made up their minds based on the color of a man's suit.

"I'll see you in the morning, Brad."

When I returned to the car, Kelly was gone. I looked down the street, both ways, as far as my eyes would see. My mind automatically began searching for the closest bar. I waited twenty minutes, and then thirty minutes, afraid to leave. Finally she walked up from behind and got in the car. She'd been crying.

"Where have you been? I've been waiting for a half hour."

She kept her face turned away like a child. Trying to hide the redness.

"I just went for a walk. Can we go home now?"

We rode in silence until we arrived outside my apartment.

"I'm going to the office to get some work done. I'll see you later tonight."

Kelly got out of the car and walked slowly away. I just wanted to get to the office, pour a glass of whiskey, steady myself. I just wanted to dig back through the file one last time. Maybe find that one thing I missed. That one word in a police report, or notation on the autopsy diagrams. But two drinks later, I hadn't even opened the file. And after the third cool whiskey, I couldn't go home.

On the way to Buddy's Bar & Grill I thought about Kelly at home alone. My favorite barstool was unoccupied, and I plopped my tired ass down next to a lady who looked eighty years old, submerged in a fog of cigarette smoke.

From behind the counter Lola said, "If it ain't Lawyer Jack. We watched you on the news tonight. Give up some dirty details."

"How 'bout a drink instead?"

Lola looked at the old lady and said, "Watch out, granny. When Bull Jack Skinner gets drunk, he won't take no for an answer. Cross your legs, honey." Lola laughed.

I turned and looked point blank at the old lady. She looked like she'd spent her entire life at the bar, smoking cigarettes, eating stale pretzels, drinking alcohol until her insides were bleached white as cotton. She crossed her legs and the movement sent my mind in the direction of the creature buried in her pants. How long had it been since someone wanted her? Anyone?

The old lady said, "You keep yo gun in yo holsta, cowboy."

I sat at that fuckin' bar half the night, next to that drunk old lady, wondering how, of all the places in the whole wide world, in the history of the human race, I ended up at Buddy's Bar & Grill at two-thirty in the morning with the devil's idiot sister. Maybe she wondered the same thing. Our conversation reminded me of Yosemite Sam.

I finally found the strength and courage to leave. On the way home I came to a traffic light. It was red, and I stopped. As far as I could see to the right, and the left, and straight ahead, there was no one. There were no car lights, no people, not even a stray dog. I sat and waited, the light glowing red.

You can tell a lot about a person from how long

they'll wait at a red light at two-thirty in the morning with no one around. I looked left, and right, and straight ahead again. There were no cops, no sign of danger, and I sat anyway, drunk as a goat, waiting for a red light to change in the middle of nowhere.

Someone once told me that our eyes see in curves. If people were physically able to have vision without limitation of distance, we could actually see the backs of our own heads. That night, sitting alone at the stop light, I caught a glimpse of the back of my own head. I don't remember driving home after that.

CHAPTER 26

Investigator Randy Riley took the witness stand. He carried with him a large brown file folder and a few evidence bags. I expected he would be the State's first witness and their last, laying the foundation of the case at the beginning and trying to wrap it all together at the end.

Riley related how he was called to the scene, who was present, and a brief description of what he saw before the crime scene videotape was popped into the machine. I objected to allowing the jury to hear the audio, and we all sat in silence watching the eerie film. I had watched it several times before, and made the proper objections.

We saw the front door open as the investigator holding the camera slowly moved down a hallway. The view turned into the living room and there were immediate signs of chaos. Haddie Charles was stretched across the carpet, one shoe on and one shoe off. A chair was turned over and the telephone was on the floor next to the body. The camera aimed at one side of the room and then inched slowly past framed family photos, a bookshelf, the fireplace, ending on the dead body, and then focusing on the gash in the skull of Haddie Charles facing upwards, dark blood in her light old-lady hair. If it wasn't for the blood, she might just have been taking a nap in a strange place, mouth open in slumber.

As the camera moved through different rooms, Deborah Webb asked questions to Investigator Riley describing the footage. We saw the jewelry box opened and empty. We saw the attic stairs hanging from the ceiling in a hallway. We saw the gable vent from the side of the house, removed and leaning against the inside wall of the attic. It all became very real to the twelve people in the jury box. Someone was dead. And someone had killed her.

I have read the transcript of the trial from cover to cover more occasions than I can count. I have edited, summarized, and deleted the trial testimony in order to avoid boring, irrelevant, or repetitious parts. For me, even those parts are memorized.

DEBORAH WEBB: Describe the condition of the body as you saw it.

INVESTIGATOR RILEY: Haddie Charles was on the floor, the left side of her face resting on the carpet. The right side of her head, just above the ear, was covered in blood. The blood was dry. Her purse was on the floor behind the couch, like it had been thrown back there. There were some papers and mail scattered around. The telephone was next to her body off the hook. The only prints we got from the phone were those of Haddie Charles. The ring finger on her left hand was missing. There was blood on the carpet where I assume her finger was cut off, but it wasn't much. The coroner says she was dead when the finger was cut off.

Photographs were introduced into evidence along with the videotape. The attic vent, pieces of carpet, and the jewelry box were all introduced.

DEBORAH WEBB: Were you able to determine a list of items apparently stolen?

INVESTIGATOR RILEY: Yes, as good as we could.

DEBORAH WEBB: How did you put together that list?

INVESTIGATOR RILEY: We interviewed family members, friends, the cleaning lady. People who knew her and were familiar with her belongings. We also had a full list with descriptions of the jewelry on her insurance policies along with photographs of the jewelry.

DEBORAH WEBB: And what did you determine was missing?

I didn't object to the list, even though it was mostly hearsay. There was no point in parading all those witnesses in front of the jury who were so close to Ms. Charles and could inject more emotions. Besides, the list didn't hurt our case. Brad Caine had one necklace. One. Not a million dollars worth of jewelry. And not a camera, or a brass bookend.

DEBORAH WEBB: Besides the jewelry, was anything else missing?

INVESTIGATOR RILEY: There could be other things missing, but we know for sure her camera is gone. She had it earlier that day taking pictures with a friend down by the beach. We've never recovered the camera. There was also a missing brass bookend and some cash. We're not sure how much.

DEBORAH WEBB: Did you look for fingerprints in the house?

INVESTIGATOR RILEY: We did. We tried to locate prints on the doorknobs, some windows, the telephone, furniture, the jewelry box.

DEBORAH WEBB: And did you find any?

INVESTIGATOR RILEY: Yes. Most of them matched Ms. Charles or the cleaning lady. We found quite a few smudged prints or partials that couldn't be identified.

DEBORAH WEBB: Did you find any fingerprints of the defendant?

INVESTIGATOR RILEY: No, ma'am. We didn't.

DEBORAH WEBB: Which leads me to my next question. When Mr. Caine was arrested in his motel room, did you recover any gloves?

INVESTIGATOR RILEY: Yes, ma'am.

DEBORAH WEBB: Tell me about that.

INVESTIGATOR RILEY: The motel room had a drop ceiling. Up in the ceiling we found a pair of rubber gloves. They were still wet. He'd been in the room since Monday at 10:00 a.m., and he was arrested Wednesday.

The rubber gloves were sealed in a plastic bag. They were introduced into evidence and passed around with the photographs from juror to juror. I watched Larry

Foley thumb through the pictures and then pass them along. He shot me a look like I had some work to do.

DEBORAH WEBB: Were you able to locate any witnesses in the neighborhood who remembered a suspicious vehicle?

INVESTIGATOR RILEY: Yes, we found two people, Ann Gilbert and Marty Corzine, who gave us a description of a vehicle, and even a partial tag.

JACK SKINNER: Objection. Any description would be hearsay.

JUDGE STEVENS: Objection sustained. The witnesses themselves will have to testify to that.

DEBORAH WEBB: Without telling us the description of the car, make, model, color, or tag number, tell me this: at the time you got the description of the car, had you ever heard of Brad Caine?

INVESTIGATOR RILEY: No, ma'am.

DEBORAH WEBB: When Brad Caine was arrested three days later, did his car match the description, make, model, color, and partial tag number?

INVESTIGATOR RILEY: Yes, ma'am, it did.

DEBORAH WEBB: And how did you get to Brad Caine in the investigation?

INVESTIGATOR RILEY: I got a call from a FBI agent telling me that a guy named Brad Caine sold a piece of the stolen jewelry on Monday, the day after the murder, to a confidential informant named Curt Junkins. It's on videotape.

DEBORAH WEBB: And then lo and behold, the same guy who's selling stolen jewelry the day after the murder has a car just like the one seen by Mrs. Gilbert and Mr. Corzine.

INVESTIGATOR RILEY: That's right.

I couldn't wait to get out of my chair. My cross-examination couldn't come soon enough. Deborah was scoring points with the jury, and Brad Caine was squirming in his seat next to me.

DEBORAH WEBB: When you arrested Brad Caine, did you read him his Miranda rights?

INVESTIGATOR RILEY: I did. He signed the waiver of rights and wrote a statement.

DEBORAH WEBB: Can you read that statement out loud for the jury?

INVESTIGATOR RILEY: "I left Birmingham at around ten-thirty or eleven o'clock at night. I drove halfway and slept in my car in a parking lot in Greenville. I drove the rest of the way the next morning and checked into the motel around ten o'clock in the morning. I met Eddie Polston outside the McDonald's in Loxley around ten-thirty. Polston gave me a necklace as payment for money I loaned him. That's all I know."

DEBORAH WEBB: So Mr. Caine says he didn't even arrive in Baldwin County until Monday morning, approximately fifteen hours after witnesses say they saw the red car?

INVESTIGATOR RILEY: That's correct.

DEBORAH WEBB: Who is Edward Polston?

INVESTIGATOR RILEY: We haven't been able to find a man named Edward Polston. From checking records we believe a man named Edward Polston lived in the county a few years ago, but we haven't been able to find him. We weren't able to find anyone who had seen him in the county the past year before the murder.

DEBORAH WEBB: Were you able to find a single witness in Birmingham to corroborate Mr. Caine's story that he didn't leave there until 10:30 or 11:00 p.m.?

INVESTIGATOR RILEY: No. We talked with a man named Phillip Ray who says he ate lunch on Sunday with Mr. Caine at around noon. We talked with eleven people in his apartment complex, but not one person saw him after that.

DEBORAH WEBB: How long is the drive from Birmingham?

INVESTIGATOR RILEY: It took us about four and a half hours.

DEBORAH WEBB: And what time Sunday evening was Haddie Charles killed?

INVESTIGATOR RILEY: We've narrowed it down to sometime between 7:30 and 8:30 p.m.

DEBORAH WEBB: Oh, by the way, did you watch Mr. Caine write his statement?

INVESTIGATOR RILEY: Yes, ma'am.

DEBORAH WEBB: Did he write it with his right hand or his left hand?

INVESTIGATOR RILEY: Left.

DEBORAH WEBB: And on which side of Haddie Charles's head was she bludgeoned to death?

INVESTIGATOR RILEY: The right.

Deborah Webb drove home her point with a swing of her left hand at Investigator Riley, an arm's length away, stopping abruptly before connecting with the right side of his head. Juries liked Deborah. She's aggressive, but not a bitch. She's able to walk that thin line female attorneys are forced to walk. I knew from experience that she liked to make a strong first impression and then follow up with witnesses and evidence to support each of her pieces of the circumstantial puzzle.

DEBORAH WEBB: Do you have the necklace that Mr. Caine was caught selling to Curt Junkins?

INVESTIGATOR RILEY: Yes, ma'am. (He held up a plastic bag containing the necklace.)

DEBORAH WEBB: After you received the videotape and the information from the FBI, what did you do?

INVESTIGATOR RILEY: We checked into Curt Junkins. He was working as a confidential informant for the FBI. I was able to find a connection between Curt Junkins and Brad Caine.

DEBORAH WEBB: And what is that connection?

I asked the court for permission to approach the bench. I didn't want to make too many objections in front of the jury, but I needed to preserve issues for appeal. I already knew the information from the prior burglaries would be introduced, but it was by far the biggest issue for appeal. After the objection was over-ruled again, Deborah Webb continued with her questioning. Brad Caine looked very uneasy. He was trying to take notes, but he was much more interested in the faces of the jurors and the growing mountain of evidence.

DEBORAH WEBB: You can answer the question. What is the connection between Curt Junkins and Brad Caine?

INVESTIGATOR RILEY: Mr. Caine was convicted of several burglaries up in Birmingham in the past. After those burglaries he sold the stolen jewelry to Junkins, who apparently is in the business of buying stolen goods.

DEBORAH WEBB: And so just as in his past crimes, Mr. Caine went to Curt Junkins?

INVESTIGATOR RILEY: That's correct.

DEBORAH WEBB: But this time Curt Junkins just happened to be working for the FBI?

INVESTIGATOR RILEY: That's correct.

DEBORAH WEBB: What other similarities did you find between Mr. Caine's past burglaries and the burglary of the home of Haddie Charles?

INVESTIGATOR RILEY: The method of entry. It is unusual.

DEBORAH WEBB: And what is that method of entry?

INVESTIGATOR RILEY: Through the gable vent on the side of the house. It was removed, and entry was made through the attic.

DEBORAH WEBB: How long have you been an investigator?

INVESTIGATOR RILEY: I've been in law enforcement seventeen years. The last six I've been an investigator.

DEBORAH WEBB: And in those seventeen years, how many burglary cases have you worked where entry was made through the side attic vent of the victim's home?

INVESTIGATOR RILEY: One.

DEBORAH WEBB: And what case is that?

INVESTIGATOR RILEY: This case. The home of Haddie Charles.

DEBORAH WEBB: And what other similarities have you found between Mr. Caine's past burglaries and this case?

INVESTIGATOR RILEY: The homes were all in neighborhoods. The stolen merchandise was always jewelry. And also, the use of gloves. Mr. Caine used gloves in all his burglaries. He was caught with gloves in Birmingham and admitted using them in the Birmingham burglaries.

My cross-examination was lengthy. It took the rest of the entire day. I asked about the brown hair found at the scene that did not match Brad's hair. I asked about the fact that they never found the rest of the jewelry or the camera anywhere, including in the car or motel room of Brad Caine. I made a big deal out of the fact that Brad Caine's fingerprints or hairs or DNA were not found on the rubber gloves. I waved around the computer printout with the list of similar cars with similar tag numbers, stretching the statistics as far as possible. I talked about how Brad Caine never hurt anyone in his past burglaries, how he had pleaded guilty to what he had done in the past, and how he sure as hell never cut off anyone's finger. I talked about how he had an accomplice in his past burglaries and always left the victims' homes neat and tidy.

JACK SKINNER: You talked about Mr. Caine being left-handed?

INVESTIGATOR RILEY: Yes.

JACK SKINNER: Well, you don't know if she was struck from behind or from in front, do you?

INVESTIGATOR RILEY: No, I don't.

JACK SKINNER: I'm left-handed. I'm sure some of the jurors are left-handed. Does that mean we're suspects?

INVESTIGATOR RILEY: No, sir. It doesn't.

JACK SKINNER: How hard did you really look for Edward Polston?

INVESTIGATOR RILEY: We ran tax records, criminal records, and we interviewed people where he used to work.

JACK SKINNER: If you ran his criminal record I'm sure you found out he had a prior arrest for assault?

INVESTIGATOR RILEY: Yes, sir. We did.

JACK SKINNER: Brad Caine doesn't have a prior arrest for assault, does he? In fact, he has no arrests for violence at all.

INVESTIGATOR RILEY: I didn't say he did.

Riley held his temper, but I felt we were able to make some headway, create some doubt, cast some uncertainty over parts of the evidence. At the end of the day I sat with Brad at the table in the courtroom. The guards stood far enough away for us to whisper. Brad was clearly shaken by what he had seen. The possibility of conviction and a death sentence was suddenly real. He mostly listened as I explained what to expect next. I saw him glance in the direction of Kelly in the back of the courtroom. I felt my blood rise.

"Do you think you might want to pay attention to this conversation?" I said sarcastically.

Brad Caine looked at me with a look I hadn't seen before. It was the first time I thought he might be capable of killing. It lasted just a moment, but I can remember it still.

CHAPTER 27

On Tuesday night, after the full day of testimony from Randy Riley, I sat at the kitchen table with the Brad Caine file spread from one end to the other. Kelly cooked dinner, rattling pans in the kitchen and talking too much.

"I thought you really pinned him down about Edward Polston. He didn't want to talk about that assault conviction."

I didn't respond.

"And the list of similar cars. That'll help a lot when those people from the neighborhood get up to testify."

She brought me a plate of baked chicken and green beans. I wasn't hungry, but I didn't want to hurt Kelly's feelings. She sat down at the table with me, no plate of her own.

"Daddy, you need to sleep in the bed tonight. You need to get a good night's sleep."

I immediately pictured the scene when I awoke to find Kelly in the bed with me, wearing only her panties.

"I'll sleep on the couch," she added.

I was unable to distinguish between relief and disappointment. I just ate my chicken.

Later, Kelly fell asleep on the couch while I worked. She had insisted on watching cartoons, the sound down low, and dozed off in the middle of Sylvester and Tweety. I looked up from my work from time to time to see the idiotic cat bust his ass repeatedly, failing to taste the meat of the sweet little yellow bird. Is every cartoon based upon the repeated efforts of a buffoon to reach the unreachable goal? What lesson is that for a child?

I slept in my own bed for the first time in quite a while. I had forgotten how comfortable it could be. At three-thirty I woke up and went to the kitchen for water. I was extra quiet, moving slowly through the darkness. The light from the television showed the way.

Kelly was gone. I picked up and dropped the empty blanket on the couch to prove it to myself. There had been a reason for her suggestion besides mere concern for my rest. I took one step toward the bedroom with intentions of dressing and going out after her, but then it occurred to me that she was a grown woman, free to come and go as she pleased. She did not belong to me, nor to anyone else.

I lay in bed listening for the sound of the front door. Listening for the squeak of the springs in the couch. At six-thirty I was finally rewarded with the noise. Fifteen minutes later I showered and dressed, wrestling the entire time with whether or not to confront Kelly. It seemed useless, but the desire to know hung like a weight around my neck. Had she gone to the bar? To meet a man? Maybe Wayne? Maybe the father of the child in her belly? There was no way to separate the emotions. They seemed perfectly normal and unnatural at the same time.

We rode to the courthouse together. She took up where she left off the night before, upbeat, almost delusional in her optimism. I decided not to ask where she'd been.

As I expected, after Investigator Riley testified, Deborah started in a direction of chronological order. Ann Gilbert was followed by Marty Corzine. Both had similar descriptions of the car, but Mrs. Gilbert provided the first three digits of the tag. She was a self-appointed neighborhood secret agent who probably spied on her neighbors. Neither of them could identify Brad Caine as the driver of the car. Neither had called the police about the so-called suspicious vehicle.

Under cross-examination, with a list shoved in their faces, both had to agree there were similar cars around the State of Alabama. Even so, it was damaging testimony. A huge coincidence that Brad's car would end up fitting the description exactly, including the partial tag number.

The real estate agent who found the body testified next. Her name was Gladys Cooper. She was supposed to drop off some paperwork to Haddie Charles at nine o'clock on Sunday night. She saw the old lady's car in the driveway and knocked on the door. Eventually she let herself in with a "yoo-hoo" warning. There was no answer. Mrs. Cooper described coming around the corner of the hallway into the living room just as we had seen through the eye of the camera the day before. Her testimony was purely for effect, no evidentiary value, and I was gentle with her.

Brad had drawn an odd-looking chart on his yellow pad intended to track the ebb and flow of the trial. It had the appearance of a stock market graph, rising and falling with each phase of the trial. I found myself sneaking a peek from time to time to see how we were doing.

The doctor who performed the autopsy testified next.

DEBORAH WEBB: What was the cause of death of Haddie Charles?

DR. HASTINGS: Blunt force injuries to the head.

DEBORAH WEBB: Did you determine this was a homicide?

DR. HASTINGS: Absolutely. She didn't die of natural causes, and in my opinion this wasn't a suicide.

DEBORAH WEBB: Can you tell what she was hit with?

DR. HASTINGS: Well, a brass bookend was submitted for analysis. Apparently a matching bookend was missing. It was consistent with the wound. There was a single blow with enough force to kill her.

DEBORAH WEBB: Did you find any other injuries to the body?

DR. HASTINGS: Her ring finger on the left hand was cut off just above the bottom knuckle. The wound was jagged, like a saw or a serrated knife was used. The finger wasn't recovered, so I was unable to examine the missing piece.

DEBORAH WEBB: Did Ms. Charles have any alcohol or drugs

in her system when she died?

DR. HASTINGS: No, ma'am. The toxicology tests were neg-
ative for alcohol or drugs. She had eaten dinner shortly
before her death, and the contents of her stomach were
partially undigested.

DEBORAH WEBB: Are you able to give us an estimate of the
time of death?

DR. HASTINGS: Considering the stomach contents, the
blood, the time she was last seen, and the time her body
was found, I'd say between seven-thirty and eight-thirty
that night. I can't give you an exact time.

On cross-examination I focused on Brad Caine. We all
knew the lady was dead. The real question was who
killed her.

JACK SKINNER: Do you know who killed this lady?

DR. HASTINGS: No.

JACK SKINNER: Did you find any hair, or blood, or bodily
fluids, or fingerprints of Brad Caine on this woman's body
or in her home?

DR. HASTINGS: No.

JACK SKINNER: No murder weapon was submitted to you?

DR. HASTINGS: That's correct.

JACK SKINNER: You can't say whether the person who
killed her was right-handed or left-handed?

DR. HASTINGS: If I had to guess...

JACK SKINNER: I don't want a guess. Yes or no? Can you tell

us whether the murderer was left-handed for sure?

DR. HASTINGS: No, not for sure.

JACK SKINNER: That's all. Thank you, doctor.

The line on Brad's little chart moved slightly upwards. From what I could tell, upwards was good. I anticipated a downward turn after the next witness, the FBI agent.

DEBORAH WEBB: Who is Curt Junkins?

AGENT ROSS: Mr. Junkins was indicted federally for tax evasion and fraud. In an effort to receive a more favorable sentencing recommendation, he agreed to act as a confidential informant.

DEBORAH WEBB: What did he do as a confidential informant?

AGENT ROSS: Mr. Junkins wore a wire and arranged several meetings in a motel room which was equipped with a video camera. Brad Caine was never a target of ours. Mr. Caine just happened to call Curt Junkins while all this was going on and asked to meet him. The meeting was arranged at the motel room. Myself and several other agents were in the room next door monitoring.

DEBORAH WEBB: Was a videotape made of the meeting?

AGENT ROSS: Yes, it was.

DEBORAH WEBB: Your Honor, we'd ask to play the tape for the jury, both audio and video.

We all sat and watched the tape from start to finish.

Brad watched himself on the T.V. screen like he'd never seen it before. When the tape ended, Deborah Webb continued her questioning.

DEBORAH WEBB: Who called who to set up the meeting?

AGENT ROSS: Mr. Caine called Mr. Junkins. I happened to be in the room when the call came through, and I listened on the other phone.

DEBORAH WEBB: Did you know at the time that the jewelry was stolen from Haddie Charles, that there was a connection to this murder case in Baldwin County?

AGENT ROSS: No, I didn't.

DEBORAH WEBB: How long has Curt Junkins been in the south Alabama area?

AGENT ROSS: He was up in Birmingham a few years ago. He's been down here since then.

DEBORAH WEBB: Toward the middle of the tape, what does Brad Caine say about more jewelry?

AGENT ROSS: He says, "If you've got the money, there might be more." Those were his words.

DEBORAH WEBB: How did Curt Junkins pay for the stolen jewelry?

AGENT ROSS: He paid with marked fifty dollar and hundred dollar bills provided by the FBI.

DEBORAH WEBB: Did you recover this money later?

AGENT ROSS: After we reported this to the Gulf Shores Police, Investigator Riley, we later accompanied

Investigator Riley and the sheriff's department to arrest
Mr. Caine at a motel in Loxley, Alabama. The marked
money was recovered from the motel room.

Cross-examination:

JACK SKINNER: You were in the motel room when Mr. Caine
was arrested?

AGENT ROSS: Yes.

JACK SKINNER: He had no warning, no time to go hide
things, did he?

AGENT ROSS: Not that we know of.

JACK SKINNER: Yet you didn't find any more jewelry at all,
did you?

AGENT ROSS: No.

JACK SKINNER: Or a murder weapon?

AGENT ROSS: No.

JACK SKINNER: Or a 35-millimeter camera?

AGENT ROSS: No.

JACK SKINNER: Or a finger, or a hacksaw?

AGENT ROSS: No.

JACK SKINNER: In fact, for all you know, he was given that
necklace by someone else?

AGENT ROSS: Well, it's not my investigation. I couldn't say
where he got it.

JACK SKINNER: And you couldn't say who killed Haddie
Charles, you weren't there?

AGENT ROSS: No, I wasn't there.

JACK SKINNER: Do you know Edward Polston?

AGENT ROSS: No. I don't know who that is.

JACK SKINNER: Did the Gulf Shores Police ask the FBI to help locate Edward Polston, the man we believe killed Haddie Charles, stole her jewelry, gave one necklace to Brad Caine, and skipped out? Did they request the FBI's assistance to locate him nationally?

AGENT ROSS: No, not that I know of.

JACK SKINNER: So, let me understand this. The Gulf Shores Police accept your help handing them a suspect on a silver platter, Brad Caine, but don't need your help investigating other suspects?

AGENT ROSS: You'll have to ask the Gulf Shores Police.

JACK SKINNER: That's all. Thank you, Agent Ross.

Judge Stevens decided to break for the day. After the jury left there was a discussion concerning the expected length of the trial. It was Wednesday, and based on Deborah Webb's estimate, she would rest her case near the middle of the next day. We'd probably be doing closing arguments by Friday afternoon if Brad testified.

I was curious to get a look at Brad's homemade trial chart. Sitting at the table together, I pulled his yellow legal pad in front of me.

"What's this?"

Brad explained, "Well, I'm just trying to get an idea of what the jury might be feeling. After each little part of the case, starting with the opening arguments, I move the line on the graph up or down depending on how it went for us."

I could see how the jagged line moved downward after Deborah's opening statement, and then back upwards after my opening argument. The graph reminded me how differently a normal person sees the court process. I would have no perspective to make such a chart. I wouldn't be able to separate the legal issues from the factual issues, the emotions from the competition.

"What's this solid line through the middle of the graph?" I asked.

"I guess that's the guilty line. Whenever we're above that line, we're in the not guilty range. Whenever we dip below, I figure the jury is leaning toward guilty."

After the FBI agent's testimony, the graph was slightly below the "guilty line." Brad was afraid. It was on his face.

"It's not over yet, Brad."

"I know," he answered.

CHAPTER 28

I woke up Thursday morning to the sound of thunder rolling in the distance. I stopped by the office on the way to court to pick up my old gray raincoat. My mind was completely and totally occupied with the trial. The office seemed like a foreign place.

The night before, I'd called Brad's boss, Ray Sherman, to ask him to come to court to testify. He had good things to say about Brad and could help us paint a picture of a man working hard to leave his past problems behind, working toward the dream of owning his own sports bar. I had also called Phillip Ray, the friend Brad had lunch with in Birmingham around noontime on the day Haddie Charles was killed. I figured Deborah would rest her case Thursday afternoon, and we'd have time for a few short defense witnesses. They could give the jurors something to think about during the night before Brad would testify Friday morning.

Curt Junkins took the stand. A bearded, large man, with a cocky edge and droopy eyes.

DEBORAH WEBB: Did you know Brad Caine before you met

with him in the motel room to buy the necklace?

CURT JUNKINS: Yeah, we go way back.

DEBORAH WEBB: How'd you know him?

CURT JUNKINS: Six, seven years ago, somethin' like that, Brad used to come to me with jewelry.

DEBORAH WEBB: Stolen jewelry?

CURT JUNKINS: Yeah, stolen. He was hittin' houses up in Birmingham and gettin' some pretty nice stuff.

DEBORAH WEBB: What happened?

CURT JUNKINS: He got caught, and that woman he was with gave my name, and anybody else's name she could think of.

DEBORAH WEBB: Did you go to prison?

CURT JUNKINS: No, not for that.

DEBORAH WEBB: On this occasion that we're here about today, why were you working with the FBI?

CURT JUNKINS: I got arrested for tax fraud. My lawyer cut some deal with the U.S. Attorney's office. As part of the deal I had to wear a wire. They were after two guys from Florida. We were in the middle of settin' somethin' up with those guys when Caine called me outta the blue.

DEBORAH WEBB: What happened?

CURT JUNKINS: He called, said he had a necklace. The call was taped. Knowin' Brad, I figured it was stolen. So they told me just to meet with him. I bought the necklace.

DEBORAH WEBB: He called you?

CURT JUNKINS: Yeah, he called me.

DEBORAH WEBB: How'd you pay for the necklace?

CURT JUNKINS: I used FBI money.

DEBORAH WEBB: Did you know where the necklace came from?

CURT JUNKINS: Not then. Later I heard it came from that old lady's house in Gulf Shores.

DEBORAH WEBB: Did he say anything about other jewelry?

CURT JUNKINS: He just said there was more. I didn't ask him about it.

DEBORAH WEBB: Pass the witness.

I ripped into Junkins. He was fair game. A convicted felon, cocky, and a bit of a smartass. I made him go through each of his felony convictions and the details of his federal indictment. I drove home points about his "special deal" with the FBI. Then I backed off, lulled him into a little cooperation in order to utilize some information Junior Miflin had gathered.

JACK SKINNER: Before you met with Brad in your motel room, it had been a long time since you'd heard from him?

CURT JUNKINS: Yeah, since Birmingham.

JACK SKINNER: Before, when Brad sold you jewelry, did he just bring one piece at a time?

CURT JUNKINS: No, usually he'd bring a whole bag, everything he got from a house. He just wanted it out of his hands.

JACK SKINNER: But this time, he only had one necklace?

CURT JUNKINS: Yeah.

JACK SKINNER: And he didn't set up another meeting before he left?

CURT JUNKINS: Nope, sure didn't. I figured maybe that's all he had. And he was blowin' smoke about havin' more just to get the best price on the one necklace.

I paused, let the jury digest the thought, and then moved slowly along in another direction.

JACK SKINNER: You ever heard of Edward Polston?

CURT JUNKINS: Name sounds familiar. What's he look like?

JACK SKINNER: (I handed him a photograph.) This is a mugshot.

CURT JUNKINS: No. I don't think I've seen him before. Who is he?

JACK SKINNER: This is the guy Brad says gave him the necklace to pay an old debt. That's why Brad only had the one piece of jewelry. This is the guy who killed Haddie Charles.

I held the photograph up in the air for the jury to see. Deborah objected, as I knew she would, but I was done with Curt Junkins. He left the witness stand and was replaced by the investigator from Birmingham, Mark Penry.

DEBORAH WEBB: How many burglaries was Brad Caine arrested for in Birmingham?

INVESTIGATOR PENRY: Eleven. He was arrested for eleven, pled guilty to three but gave a statement as part of the plea agreement that he committed all eleven. There were another five he was never arrested for.

DEBORAH WEBB: Out of those eleven, how many were homes in residential neighborhoods?

INVESTIGATOR PENRY: All eleven.

DEBORAH WEBB: How many homes were entered through the gable vent into the attic?

INVESTIGATOR PENRY: Ten.

DEBORAH WEBB: Is that an unusual form of entry?

INVESTIGATOR PENRY: I've been at this twenty-two years, and I can't remember seeing it before. I've seen it one time since then, but the guy fell through the ceiling and broke his leg. He got caught.

DEBORAH WEBB: Out of those eleven homes, how many had jewelry stolen?

INVESTIGATOR PENRY: Ten. One lady had packed all her jewelry up and was in the process of moving out.

DEBORAH WEBB: Out of the ten burglaries where jewelry was stolen, how many times did Brad Caine sell it to Curt Junkins?

INVESTIGATOR PENRY: At least seven, according to Caine and Junkins.

DEBORAH WEBB: Did you ever get any fingerprints from the houses to match Caine?

INVESTIGATOR PENRY: No, ma'am. We knew he was in each of the houses. He told us so. But he wore gloves every time. Different gloves.

DEBORAH WEBB: Did he ever wear rubber gloves?

INVESTIGATOR PENRY: Yes, he did. We recovered a pair under his car seat, and he verified they were used.

DEBORAH WEBB: As an investigator with twenty-two years of experience, if you worked a burglary in a residential neighborhood, with entry through the side attic vent of the house, where a large amount of jewelry was stolen, and the jewelry was later sold to Curt Junkins, and rubber gloves were worn, what would be the first thing you would do?

INVESTIGATOR PENRY: I'd be knockin' on Brad Caine's door.

As I rose to cross-examine Mr. Penry, I caught a side-ways glance at Brad's chart. The line had taken a sharp downward turn after the direct testimony of Investigator Penry. In Brad's mind we were now well below the water line, holding our breath for something good to happen.

JACK SKINNER: Out of those eleven burglaries, how many people got hurt?

INVESTIGATOR PENRY: None.

JACK SKINNER: How many people got killed?

INVESTIGATOR PENRY: None.

JACK SKINNER: How many had a camera stolen?

INVESTIGATOR PENRY: None.

JACK SKINNER: How many did Brad Caine do alone?

INVESTIGATOR PENRY: None. Gracie Patrick was with him.

JACK SKINNER: And out of those eleven, how many did he deny doing?

INVESTIGATOR PENRY: He admitted to all of them right after he got caught. So did she.

JACK SKINNER: And so, as an investigator of twenty-two years, if I told you we had a burglary where the intruder acted alone, where the owner of the house was brutally murdered, where a camera was stolen, and where Brad Caine says he didn't do it, would Brad Caine be your only suspect?

INVESTIGATOR PENRY: No. An investigator has to consider all the possibilities. But he'd certainly be one of the suspects.

JACK SKINNER: Do you know Edward Polston?

INVESTIGATOR PENRY: I don't think so.

JACK SKINNER: Was he ever a suspect in the murder of Haddie Charles?

INVESTIGATOR PENRY: I don't know. It's not my investigation.

JACK SKINNER: That's all.

The line on the graph moved slightly upwards, but not as far as I would have hoped. Randy Riley finished the State's case by tying up a few evidentiary loose ends and introducing various evidence and photographs not previously introduced. The State rested its case, and I made the proper motions outside the presence of the jury. I was having a difficult time reading Larry Foley. I decided he might just be hiding his loyalty, but I must admit, I was way beyond the point of clear perspective.

I called Phillip Ray as our first defense witness.

JACK SKINNER: Did Brad seem distracted or nervous at lunch, like a man on a tight time schedule to drive to Baldwin County and kill someone?

PHILLIP RAY: No, he seemed normal. We just ate lunch.

JACK SKINNER: Was his car packed?

PHILLIP RAY: I didn't see any luggage or anything. I knew he'd been spending some weekends in Baldwin County, but he didn't mention anything at lunch.

JACK SKINNER: How do you know Brad Caine?

PHILLIP RAY: We worked together at Products, Inc. We played basketball after work once a week.

Deborah asked Mr. Ray questions about Brad's past, but he knew nothing. The witness stuck with his story that they finished lunch between noon and twelve-thirty. He didn't see Brad again, and Deborah counted the hours out loud on her fingers to show Brad Caine had plenty of time to be down in Gulf Shores by seven-thirty that night.

The last witness of the day was Ray Sherman. A short go-getter of a man who loved his job as Regional Manager of Products, Inc. He explained that the company sold various "hot" products and each Regional Manager had six full-time salesmen assigned to different territories.

JACK SKINNER: What kind of a worker was Brad Caine?

RAY SHERMAN: Always on time. Always wherever he said he would be. He started slowly, learning the sales business, but caught on quickly. We target businesses. If you deliver a good product, at a good price, people will respond. Brad had a lot of happy customers.

JACK SKINNER: And do you sell things like clocks, paperweights?

RAY SHERMAN: Yes, sir, cuckoo clocks, Civil War commemorative framed prints, many, many items. Through the years it's hard to remember all of our product lines. Brad was my salesman of the quarter, twice. I watch my guys closely for burnout. This is a high burnout business. I never saw any of the signs with Brad. He was upbeat, positive.

Deborah again attacked with questions about Brad's past criminal history.

DEBORAH WEBB: Don't you think it is a little irresponsible to hire a convicted serial burglar as a salesman?

RAY SHERMAN: We believe in giving a man a second chance. I never saw anything out of line with Brad.

DEBORAH WEBB: Why was he moving to Baldwin County?

RAY SHERMAN: I wasn't aware of that. His territory was still east of Birmingham. He asked for a few days off, and I gave it to him. He didn't mention where he was going. We talked a few times about Brad wanting to someday have his own business.

DEBORAH WEBB: Would you be surprised to know he'd packed up everything in his apartment?

RAY SHERMAN: Yes, I suppose I would. He hadn't given me any notice of quitting his job.

And the day was done, good or bad. It was Thursday afternoon. There was comfort in the thought that by Friday afternoon, one day away, the trial would be over. Brad didn't seem to share in the comfort.

I said to Brad, "I'm goin' back to the office to do some work. We'll meet early in the morning before you testify. I'll have a big list of questions we can review. You need to go over all your notes."

Brad rubbed his face in his hands.

I asked, "How we doin' on the chart?"

"I can't tell anymore."

"You've lost track, lost perspective. You're inside of it now, Brad. We can't see what the jurors see, or hear what they hear. We're just a few feet away, but it might as well be a million miles."

CHAPTER 29

The ride home was quiet. Kelly stared out the window at the heavy rain falling across the stretches of farmland. My mind was running in different directions. Brad's testimony, and maybe then Junior Miflin's, and closing arguments. Friday would be our day, our chance to move the line on the chart in the right direction. A chance to give Larry Foley and possibly other jurors something to hold onto. I dropped off Kelly at the apartment and drove alone to the office. Rose's car was still parked in the back, and I wondered why she was there past closing time. The pile on my desk was large. There was a stack of bills, unopened, on the corner. Rose was on the phone. I heard her hang up and knock gently on the open door to my office. She sat down in the client chair across the desk.

"I need to talk to you, Jack."

"I know, Rose, I know. Things will get better, I promise. Just let me get past this trial."

She looked tired, older than I'd noticed before. She also looked fed-up, resolved.

"No, Jack. Things won't get better. I've got to look out

for myself. I appreciate what you've done for me, giving me a place to work, putting up with me all these years, but I can't pay my bills. I can't live like this anymore."

I didn't argue with her. I just listened.

"I've got another job. I'll stay the next two weeks, help you find somebody to take my place."

We both knew we wouldn't find anybody to take her place. We couldn't find anybody to work for nothing, long hours, and cover my ass at every turn. We both knew a young secretary wouldn't last a week, and anyone with experience would see the warning signs. We just sat for a moment. My mind drifted to the trial, to the beginning sentences of my closing argument. I felt the adrenaline rise slightly at the thought of the courtroom, all eyes on my every movement, each word flying through the air, captured by every ear. I heard Rose speak again, but I wasn't listening.

"I'm sorry, Jack."

She stood and left the room. I heard her footsteps, and the back door close, and Rose's car start and move away. I poured myself a drink and opened the Brad Caine file. I should have told Rose he wasn't guilty, we were fighting the good fight, just hold on a few more days. Take some time off. But it wouldn't have mattered. She had made up her mind, and there was a part of me that was proud of her for having the guts to leave. It's not easy to leave. The older we get, the more frightening the unknown seems. It's not actually any more frightening, it just seems that way.

I made a list on the legal pad for Brad. A list of questions, answers, and possible problems. I was confident he would do well. Around ten-thirty I left the office and headed home. I wasn't hungry, and passed Buddy's Bar & Grill without temptation. Echo was standing at the front door. She was wet. I opened the unlocked door and stepped inside with the cat darting past.

"Jesus, Kelly, why didn't you let the cat in?" I said. But Kelly wasn't in the living room or the kitchen. I took off my coat and set the fat file down on the table. The television was on. I heard the roadrunner say, "Beep, beep," as he took off full speed down a long desert dirt road. The coyote shot an arrow, missing the road-runner. The arrow ricocheted off a big rock, flew back across the road, and landed stiff in the coyote's ass.

I heard myself say to the coyote, "Why? Why don't you just eat a lizard, or a rabbit? They're delicious."

Kelly wasn't in the bedroom. While I was changing clothes, standing in my boxer shorts, I heard a faint sound. A mumble. Coming from the bathroom. The door to the bathroom was cracked open, and it was dark inside. I stopped and listened at the crack.

It was the voice of a child, singing the words of a child's song. There was rhythm to the words, but I didn't recognize the song at first. I eased the door open and turned on the light.

There was a body curled up in the corner between the tub and the commode. The body was naked, sitting upright, rocking slightly with the rhythm of the song. I know it sounds strange, but for a long few seconds I didn't recognize Kelly. She seemed so small on the floor. So out of place. There were no pill bottles around her. No needles.

"Kelly?" I whispered. "Kelly?"

There was no answer. Kelly's head was folded between her knees, hands across the back of her neck. I walked to the edge of the tub and sat down. I slowly reached my hand to her leg. It was cold, like the leg of a mannequin. I found my eyes on her skin, her exposed breast on the side, and I put my hand to my face, squeezing my eyes closed, holding them closed, listening to the hum, the soft words.

"Hush little baby, don't say a word, Daddy's gonna buy you a mockingbird, and if that mockingbird don't sing, Daddy's gonna buy you a diamond ring..."

She would stop mid-sentence, and take off at another place, humming the melody so softly in between I could barely separate the words from the sound.

"Kelly," I said again.

She lifted her head, hands pressed on each side of her face, and looked straight into my eyes. There were dark streaks down her face from dry tears and makeup, like little riverbeds. We held the stare, and God help me, we were together inside a single memory. It seemed longer than it could possibly have been. Longer than the twenty-five years since it started.

Kelly rose from the floor, her back sliding up against the wall until the fullness of her belly was at my eyes and her nakedness was her only testimony. And then she walked away into the bedroom leaving me alone. Truly and totally alone except for the blackness that held me suspended from the rest of the world. Held me physically from moving until I heard the television turn off and the squeak of the springs in the old couch.

Echo found me in the bathroom. She sat down next to my leg and rubbed her muzzle against my skin until she purred, satisfied by the contact. I touched her on the top of the head, and the touch itself seemed to give me the energy to stand and walk to the bed, where I stayed until morning, in and out of sleep, waiting to be back in the courtroom where I belonged.

CHAPTER 30

Kelly cooked breakfast like nothing had ever happened. Ever. We sat at the table together while the rain continued to beat against the window. I politely pretended to eat, my stomach squeezed like a fist. We rode together to the courthouse. It was the final day, the big finale, and the newspaper reporters and T.V. faces would be back. They would stick around for the defendant's testimony, the closing arguments, and the verdict if it arrived in time. I met with Brad in the holding cell behind the courtroom. He listened to my questions and shook his head in reply if necessary. We had discussed this day a thousand times, but now it was here.

I explained, "And I need you to tell why you were down here, the idea of your own business, the American dream. Looking for a location, a place to live, the same reason you'd been down those other weekends."

"O.K."

"Don't waver from your story. Don't let her set you up. You might think you're making just a little change, just to patch up one question, but it's the next question to worry about. It may be the tenth question down the line before you realize the little tiny change you made has caused a very big problem.

"I'll object if I need to, but don't turn to me for protection. It's cross-examination of a defendant. Almost anything goes, Brad."

He looked at me, a young man, nearly the age of my son. He could have been my son.

"I'm ready, Mr. Skinner. I'll try to remember everything you taught me. I think I understand the air of believability. What was it you said? It's the way a man holds himself. Confident. Not over-confident. I've still got faith in the system. By tomorrow, Saturday at the latest, I'll be walking out the door a free man."

Brad Caine smiled. It was a nervous smile, but still, it was good to see.

The courtroom was nearly full. I spotted Kelly near the back. She turned her head to look at the man next to her, and I could see the ponytail hanging down her back. My mind flashed to the night before, and then back to the courtroom. The jurors were brought in. I caught the eye again of Larry Foley, and he held the look long enough to let me know his thoughts. "Give me something, Jack Skinner." That's what he would have said if he could have. Maybe Brad Caine was right, I thought. Maybe he would walk out the door a free man.

I stood. "Your Honor, we'll call Brad Caine to the witness stand."

He walked slowly across the courtroom, placed his hand on the black Bible, and took the oath.

JACK SKINNER: Tell us your name, please.

BRAD CAINE: Brad Caine.

JACK SKINNER: How old are you?

BRAD CAINE: Thirty-one.

JACK SKINNER: Before you were arrested, where did you work?

BRAD CAINE: Products, Inc. Mr. Sherman was my boss.

JACK SKINNER: What did you do?

BRAD CAINE: I was a salesman. We sold various products, gifts, things like that. I went through a training period and then got my own territory. Without bragging, I got pretty good at it.

JACK SKINNER: During the few months before you were arrested, did you travel down to Baldwin County?

BRAD CAINE: Yes, sir. I was thinking about moving down here, starting my own business. It's a nice area, and I was ready for a change, but I didn't want to just jump in the middle of it without doing my homework.

JACK SKINNER: On the weekend Haddie Charles was killed, what did you do?

BRAD CAINE: I worked on Friday, and then on Saturday I started packing up my things. I was planning to give Mr. Sherman a two-week notice, but my lease was almost up, and I didn't want to wait until the last minute to pack. I spent Saturday night at home.

JACK SKINNER: Did you have lunch with Mr. Ray on Sunday?

BRAD CAINE: Yes, sir. We met and ate lunch. He's right, we finished between noon and twelve-thirty. I went back to my apartment to pack up boxes. It's amazing how much junk you can accumulate.

JACK SKINNER: When did you leave to head down here?

BRAD CAINE: I didn't leave until about ten-thirty or eleven that night, Sunday night. I drove halfway, like I told Mr. Riley, and slept in my car in Greenville. I was too tired to drive. I woke up the next morning and drove the rest of the way. I got to the motel in Loxley and checked in around ten o'clock Monday morning. I was planning to take a few days to find myself a place to live down here and get an attorney to help me set up my business.

JACK SKINNER: So, when Haddie Charles was killed that Sunday night, between seven-thirty and eight-thirty, where were you?

BRAD CAINE: I was at home in my T-shirt cleaning the apartment and filling cardboard boxes.

JACK SKINNER: After you checked in the motel, where did you go?

BRAD CAINE: I had a meeting with a guy named Edward Polston. He owed me five hundred dollars I loaned him, and we met at the McDonald's in Loxley at about ten-thirty. We just stood out in the parking lot and talked.

JACK SKINNER: Did he pay you what he owed?

BRAD CAINE: No. He'd been making promises for months. I needed the money to help make my move. He told me he had a necklace that belonged to his wife, but he said he'd give it to me as payment. I didn't want to take it. I wasn't even sure it was real, but I figured it was better than nothing.

JACK SKINNER: Do you know where Edward Polston is now?

BRAD CAINE: No. I guess when he heard about me getting arrested, he took off. I've got no idea where he is, but I wish I did. Maybe I wouldn't be sitting here with my life on the line.

Brad was good. He was calm, matter-of-fact, and added small details to his story that made it even more believable.

JACK SKINNER: Where'd you go after you met with Mr. Polston?

BRAD CAINE: I went to your office to discuss my business ideas.

JACK SKINNER: Then what?

BRAD CAINE: I spent the afternoon driving around looking at houses and apartments to rent. I decided to call Curt Junkins to try to sell the necklace. I know it was stupid, but he was the only person I could think of in the jewelry business. We met at his motel room in Mobile. And by the way, he was right, I know how he operates. If he thought there might be more jewelry, he'd give me a better price on the necklace. Of course, I didn't have any more, but he didn't know that.

JACK SKINNER: How'd you know Curt Junkins?

BRAD CAINE: Back in my stupid days, when I was younger, I got mixed up with drugs. To pay for the drugs I broke into some houses in Birmingham. It was wrong, and I paid the price for it. I went to prison, which is what I deserved. I admitted what I did to the judge. But I didn't kill this lady. I swear to God I didn't. I haven't taken drugs or broken the law since the day I got caught in Birmingham. I swear to God.

JACK SKINNER: When were you arrested?

BRAD CAINE: Wednesday morning. In my motel room. I was planning to check out and get back to Birmingham to see Mr. Sherman. He had given me permission to take a few personal days.

JACK SKINNER: What about the rubber gloves?

BRAD CAINE: They're not mine. I don't know how they got in the ceiling. Maybe they were up there before I checked in, or the maid put them there. I wish I could tell you where they came from. I only know they aren't mine.

JACK SKINNER: Was your car down in Gulf Shores on the Sunday Haddie Charles was killed?

BRAD CAINE: No. It's not possible. I was in my car. I may have driven through that area on Monday afternoon, the next day, when I was looking for places to rent. But there's no way anyone saw me or my car in Baldwin County before I drove here Monday morning. With all due respect, those people saw someone else driving a car like mine. They didn't see me.

There comes a time for a lawyer to stop asking questions and sit down. That time had come.

JACK SKINNER: Brad, please answer Ms. Webb's questions.

The reporters were furiously writing notes, and the big black camera at the courtroom window was focused on the young man on the witness stand. I sat down. Brad's yellow legal pad was opened to the silly little chart. There was an asterisk at the stopping point the day before. It was well below the guilty line. I was tempted to add a new line to the chart, straight upwards, showing Brad's direct testimony. I just left it alone.

DEBORAH WEBB: Mr. Caine, please name all the people you spoke to on the telephone or saw in person from the time you left lunch with Phillip Ray until you say you drove to Baldwin County, ten or eleven hours later.

Brad bent his head in thought. He shook his head slowly from side to side.

BRAD CAINE: I don't think I talked to anybody, or saw anybody. I was alone, packing up everything, watching television. I ate leftovers around eight o'clock.

DEBORAH WEBB: Not one single person? Not one who saw you in the parking lot when you left? Or stopped by to say hello? Or called you on the phone?

BRAD CAINE: No ma'am. I couldn't have asked any of the guys at work to help me pack. They didn't even know I was planning to leave. And the phone in the apartment was already disconnected.

DEBORAH WEBB: Give me just one name, one person, who

saw you sleeping in the parking lot in Greenville.

BRAD CAINE: I don't know anybody in Greenville. I just parked and went to sleep. It was late.

DEBORAH WEBB: Don't you think that's just too convenient?

BRAD CAINE: I wish someone had seen me.

DEBORAH WEBB: So do I, Mr. Caine. Tell me this. How did you know Edward Polston?

BRAD CAINE: I don't remember when I met him. It was a long time ago.

DEBORAH WEBB: And you loaned him five hundred dollars? For what?

BRAD CAINE: I don't know for what. He said he needed it.

DEBORAH WEBB: So you just had five hundred dollars laying around to loan a guy that you can't even remember meeting?

BRAD CAINE: I guess so.

DEBORAH WEBB: And now, conveniently, he's disappeared.

BRAD CAINE: I guess so.

Brad was getting a little rattled. There were no more small details to this part of the story. He touched his face with his hand, and I looked directly at Larry Foley.

DEBORAH WEBB: And so this man, who owes you money, gives you a necklace in the McDonald's parking lot?

BRAD CAINE: It was better than nothing.

DEBORAH WEBB: When did he call you? We can check the

phone company records.

BRAD CAINE: I think he called from a pay phone.

DEBORAH WEBB: Technology is a wonderful thing, Mr. Caine. We can check the phone records to verify this call you say you received.

Brad was in a corner, and Deborah knew it. She would keep pushing until something happened. Brad's face began to change. He looked to me and then back at Deborah Webb.

BRAD CAINE: I can't remember exactly when he called. I can't remember if he called me at home or work.

DEBORAH WEBB: That's convenient. Don't you think?

Brad didn't answer.

DEBORAH WEBB: And so you took this necklace to your old buddy, Curt Junkins?

BRAD CAINE: He was the only person who came to mind. I knew he had moved down here.

DEBORAH WEBB: You also knew he bought stolen jewelry?

BRAD CAINE: He bought any jewelry. He didn't care where it came from.

DEBORAH WEBB: And you told him, on videotape, that there might be more?

BRAD CAINE: I explained that already. I just wanted top dollar.

DEBORAH WEBB: Why didn't you go to a pawnshop?

BRAD CAINE: I'm not from down here. I just called Junkins.

DEBORAH WEBB: You know pawnshops have cameras in the stores and require identification. You knew there would be a paper trail, a connection between you and the stolen necklace. Didn't you?

Brad didn't answer.

DEBORAH WEBB: Did Mr. Junkins give you a receipt or an invoice?

BRAD CAINE: No.

DEBORAH WEBB: That's convenient, don't you think, no paper trail?

Brad didn't answer. I pictured the line on the graph dropping steadily.

DEBORAH WEBB: Let's talk about the rubber gloves. The wet rubber gloves in the ceiling of the motel room you'd been in for three days.

BRAD CAINE: What do you want to know?

DEBORAH WEBB: You used rubber gloves in Birmingham, didn't you?

BRAD CAINE: Yes, a few times.

DEBORAH WEBB: You used rubber gloves when you broke into those residential houses, eleven of them, entered through the side attic vent each time, stole jewelry each time, and took that jewelry to Curt Junkins. Right?

Brad looked over at me again. It was a strange look, not like he was begging for help, but like he was teetering on the edge of something and knew the moment was near. Brad Caine took a deep breath, closed his eyes for a moment, and began to slowly shake his head. The silence was impossible.

Brad looked directly at me and said, "I'm sorry, I can't do this anymore."

There was another piece of silence as we stared across the courtroom at each other. Deborah Webb turned to me, and then turned back to Brad Caine. I felt eyes upon my back and movement in the jury box.

DEBORAH WEBB: What are you talking about, Mr. Caine?

Brad said to me, "I'm sorry, but it's just not going to work. This is my life here."

I remember thinking to myself, "This is brilliant. Whatever it is, it's brilliant. He's got the courtroom on the edge of their seats. Everyone." It was a level of believability I'd never seen before. I waited. Brad turned his attention directly to the judge. He spoke calmly.

BRAD CAINE: I didn't kill this lady. Mr. Skinner hired me to get rid of the jewelry. He had a briefcase in the closet at his office. It's probably still there. A black briefcase. He opened it in front of me to get the necklace. I saw it. I saw the lady's finger in a clear sandwich bag. And more jewelry. I saw a brass bookend with blood still on it.

Brad Caine turned to Deborah Webb, the jurors transfixed against the wall.

BRAD CAINE: It's probably still in his office. Go look for yourself. I couldn't have put it there. I've been in jail six months, since the day I was arrested.

Judge Stevens interrupted. "Ladies and gentlemen of
the jury, I'm going to ask you to step outside to the jury
room. We've got some matters which have to be
addressed outside of your presence. I'll remind you, don't
speak to each other about this case. Don't allow anyone
to speak to you about it."

As I rose from my chair I remember still thinking,
"This is brilliant. Brad will have the jury so confused,
they'll never convict him. And then later, when there's
no evidence to prosecute me, double jeopardy will have
attached and Brad can never be tried for this crime
again."

After the jury left the courtroom, Judge Stevens
questioned Brad himself.

JUDGE STEVENS: If this is a stunt, Mr. Caine, I can promise
you it won't work out the way you'd like. On the record,
outside of the presence of the jury, I'm going to ask you
a few questions. Tell me about the briefcase.

BRAD CAINE: I met with Mr. Skinner at his office that
Monday morning. I wanted to hire him to help get my
record expunged so I could get a liquor license and open
a bar. In our conversation I told him about my prior criminal history. I didn't have much money to hire him. He
asked me about jewelry. Selling jewelry. He asked me
about my old contacts, and I told him about Curt Junkins
and other people. Mr. Skinner offered to do my legal
work for free if I'd arrange to sell a necklace. He said he
had some jewelry a client had given him to pay his fee,

and he needed to turn it into cash. He pulled a black briefcase out of the closet, opened it on the desk, and pulled out a necklace. I saw other jewelry, necklaces, rings, it looked like high-priced merchandise. I also saw what looked like a finger in a little plastic bag, and a brass thing, and some other stuff. Some cash.

The full weight of what was happening fell down upon me all at once. It was an amazing situation.

JACK SKINNER: Judge, I'm going to object to this. I'm going to ask to meet with my client in private. This is insanity.

JUDGE STEVENS: Jack, I think you need to sit down. If there's nothing to this, we'll figure it out. Your objection is noted and overruled.

I turned to look at the spectators. It was the first time I truly understood what it's like to be looked at the way my clients have been looked at in courtrooms my entire career, clients like Brad Caine and Gabriel Black. In the jumble of faces I saw Kelly sitting near the back of the room. Her face was blank.

JUDGE STEVENS: Did Mr. Skinner tell you where he got the jewelry?

BRAD CAINE: No, sir. He only gave me the one necklace, but he said if I sold it, we'd sell more and I'd get a cut. That's why I said what I said to Junkins. Mr. Skinner came to my motel room Tuesday morning. That's who was in the room when the maid came by. He wouldn't take the money from me. He just wanted to see it. I guess he got spooked, or maybe somebody tipped him off about the

FBI. I don't know. He just said he'd come by the next day to get the money and give me more jewelry to sell. I went into the bathroom to take a shower. I guess that's when he put the gloves up in the ceiling. That's when he started setting me up.

JUDGE STEVENS: Why would you have this man as your attorney, if he did this to you?

BRAD CAINE: He said everything would be all right. He said they'd never convict me on circumstantial evidence. Just be patient. But I'm not stupid. I can see where this is going. He wants me convicted. It's the perfect frame. I get sentenced to the death penalty, and he gets away with all the jewelry. I don't have any money. He said he'd represent me for free. I actually thought it might work, he gets me off, we split up the money. I was an idiot.

We all sat still for a moment. I glanced at Brad's chart next to me on the table. I remembered the brief-case, and the five thousand dollars cash, and everything began to come together. The son-of-a-bitch played me. How could I not have seen it coming? How could I have let it happen?

DEBORAH WEBB: Your Honor, obviously the State can't take Mr. Caine's word on this. I'm going to ask the court to recess. I'll prepare a search warrant for the office of Jack Skinner based on this information and other information gathered in the investigation.

JACK SKINNER: Judge, this is ridiculous. Again, I'm going to object and ask that I be allowed to speak to my client.

We're in the middle of a capital murder trial, for God's sake.

DEBORAH WEBB: Judge, I'm going to object to Mr. Skinner meeting with his client. At this point, we don't know who could be charged. I'm going to ask that Mr. Skinner be ordered to turn over his cell phone to the court so he cannot call his office. I'm going to ask that he be detained until the investigators can execute the search warrant.

JUDGE STEVENS: Jack, give your cell phone to the bailiff. I'm going to allow you to meet with your client in the holding cell, but you won't be allowed to leave here.

JACK SKINNER: This is ridiculous, Judge.

JUDGE STEVENS: Maybe, but we're going to do this my way. Court is adjourned.

The reporters bolted from their chairs and ran out of the courtroom to get their stories on air or in print. The big black camera at the courtroom door turned to me, standing alone at the defense table. I handed the bailiff my phone and walked with him to the holding cell. Brad Caine was led by a deputy to the same place. We sat down in the only two chairs available in the small room. I noticed things I hadn't noticed before. The stainless steel toilet in the corner. The sound of the heavy door closing behind us. The face of the guard peering through the little window. And there we sat, face to face, quiet for a few moments.

Brad said, "How's it feel?"

"Fuck you," was all I could say.

"No, Jack, fuck you. I figure we've got a couple of hours to chat. Let me start by telling you how it happened. You at least deserve the full story."

I listened.

"How do you suppose I knew Haddie Charles had a load of jewelry?"

I didn't answer.

"Kelly. Your daughter. You told her all about it. Who do you suppose I was coming down to see all those weekends? Kelly. Poor old Kelly. Your mess of a daughter."

"You're a lying piece of shit. Don't bring her into this."

"She brought herself into it. We met in a bar down by the beach. She was drunk. I told her I'd been to prison for stealing jewelry. Next thing I knew, she was telling me about old Haddie Charles. It seemed too good to be true.

"We went down to the house together, Jack. We went inside together. You're gonna get a kick out of this. Have you ever gotten a blow job in somebody's house, somebody's house you just broke in, with the pure excitement that someone might come home any minute, any second?"

My anger began to rise. I had to hold back. I had to tell myself that Brad Caine was just trying to get me to take a swing at him, get the guard to tackle me and drag me out. Just trying to make me react like a guilty man.

"Of course you haven't. But I have. You know, Jack, there's a thin difference between living and being alive. In the living room of Haddie Charles, Kelly was down on her knees. You should have seen her face when that old lady came around the corner of the hallway. We didn't even hear her open the door.

"And you should have seen Kelly pick up that heavy bookend from the shelf and crack that woman across the head when she went for the phone. The same bloody bookend inside the briefcase. The murder weapon. My pants were still down around my ankles."

He turned his head away from the guard to laugh softly. I just listened. There was nothing else to do.

"We loaded up the jewelry in a black briefcase I found in the back of a storage closet. The same black briefcase in your closet now with your fingerprints all over it. I bet you touched it, didn't you? The same black briefcase with a few pieces of the jewelry inside, and that poor old lady's finger I had to cut off to get that big diamond ring. The same diamond ring that put a cut above Kelly's eye when the old lady fought back. Remember that cut? The little scar above Kelly's eye when you went to see her at the shelter? Don't worry, lots of other people remember that cut, too.

"Anyway, I burned my gray service uniform I like to wear on the job, and the shoes with blood on them. I stashed most of the jewelry and used the wad of cash to pay you Monday morning. Old people love to stash money in the house. Your bank records will show how you deposited the money.

"You were just my fallback position, my safety net. I saw your letter and made sure to put it next to the body. Kelly told me about all your financial problems. It was easy. I dropped off the briefcase, got the murder weapon and the finger out of my hands, and gave you the five thousand dollars to run through your trust account.

"If everything had worked out, I just would've come back in a few weeks, picked up the briefcase, and gotten back most of the retainer. The money would be clean. How could I have known old Curt Junkins was working with the FBI? How could I have known that?

"So when the shit hit the fan, I fell back on you. Maybe if you'd have done a better job in this trial it would've never come to this. But you saw the chart. Those assholes were gonna convict me."

As he spoke, my mind searched for a crack in his story. Anything. Something he overlooked.

"I will admit I screwed up on the gloves. That was just plain stupid. I let my guard down. I washed 'em the morning I was arrested and left 'em up there. It would've been so easy to just flush them down the toilet. Maybe if I had, we wouldn't be here."

I looked up at the face of the guard at the window. It was white and square, the hair on his head crew-cut. I noticed he was focused on me, not Brad Caine.

"I know what you're thinking, Jack. But it gets even better, believe it or not. After Kelly killed that old lady, and she lay on the floor in her own blood, we fucked like dogs. Standing up, Kelly bent over the couch. I can't explain the exhilaration. I wish I could, but I can't.

"When we finished, Kelly sat down next to the old lady. I took her picture. Remember the missing camera? It's not missing at all. The film inside has a picture of your daughter next to the dead woman. And the cut on Kelly's head, her blood is still on the ring, sealed neatly in a plastic bag. They can do wonders with DNA these days. And you know the mysterious brown hair found in the living room? You're right. It's Kelly's hair."

We sat quietly for several very long minutes. He had covered every base, every little detail.

"What I'm saying, Jack, is this: if you try to fight this, if I end up on the witness stand in my case, or yours, I'm not going down alone. I'll turn over the camera, the ring with the DNA, and tell them everything.

"We both know you're a disgusting human being. Kelly told me about what you did to her. But even a disgusting human being like you wouldn't send your daughter for a lethal injection. Besides, we're gonna have a baby."

I closed my eyes and felt a lightness in my head. My rationality began to slide away, and I remember wondering if it was all a crazy dream like that dream about my father hitting me for no reason. I saw his face again, standing over me, and his arm raised. But it was no dream. It was real.

"I used everything you taught me, Jack. You were right about that air of believability. If it's any consolation, Kelly didn't know I was going to do this. She really thought her daddy could make it all O.K. She really thought you could walk me out of this courtroom, and we'd all live happily ever after."

I remember thinking, who will take care of the cat? Who will feed Echo? She wouldn't know what to do without me.

Brad said, "If it's a boy, I think we'll call him Jack. Yeah, Jack. That's a good strong name."

The cell door opened, and Deborah Webb entered.

She motioned for Brad Caine to leave with the deputy, and she sat down in the chair across from me. She was very businesslike, but the coldness in her words held a sadness. I had never paid attention to pity before.

"It's not good, Jack. They found the briefcase. Rose says she never saw Brad Caine bring the briefcase, or pay the five thousand dollars in cash you said he paid. We know all about your financial problems, and of course the letter to Haddie Charles which establishes motive.

"Jesus, Jack, the woman's finger was in the briefcase. And the jewelry inside matches the insurance photographs. And Haddie Charles's cleaning lady identified the briefcase. She just hadn't noticed it missing. The bookend matches and has dried blood on it."

I tried to look her square in the eye as she spoke, keeping my face empty of all expression. I kept my mind on Kelly, probably still sitting in the back of the courtroom, waiting for me to come out and tell her everything would be O.K.

"Jesus, Jack. I don't know how much Caine was involved in all of this, but you've got to help yourself. Where's the rest of the jewelry? Where's the camera? Where were you between seven-thirty and eight-thirty when Haddie Charles was killed?"

I hadn't thought about where I'd been at the time of the murder. It didn't make any difference anyway. My mind went back to that evening. It was almost funny. I was home, alone, probably eating a fucking cheeseburger. Why couldn't I have been at the dinner table with my wife, my children, the grandchildren? Playing Monopoly on the rug? Laughing at cartoons?

But they were stupid questions to be asking myself. I already knew the answers.

When I finally spoke, I said without remorse, "Deborah, I don't have anything to say."

It was the last time I ever spoke to her.

CHAPTER 31

There is a moment in a man's life, crystal and linear, when he sees himself for all he is, and all he is not. My attorney, acting on my instruction, negotiated a plea bargain agreement. The district attorney's office agreed not to seek the death penalty if I would plead guilty. The only other sentence available in the State of Alabama on a capital murder conviction is life in the penitentiary without the possibility of parole.

I considered other options. In jail a man has a great deal of time to think about all those things he ignored before. I've been guilty my whole life, what difference does it make what's written on the paperwork? I narrowed down the options and decided I was left with only two. The option I selected, or calling the bluff of Brad Caine. And I knew damn well it wasn't a bluff. I knew that son-of-a-bitch had the jewelry, and the camera, and the ring. And even if he was lying about taking the picture of Kelly next to the body, or the DNA on the ring, it wouldn't matter. Kelly would confess under pressure. Her hair would probably match the hair found in the living room of Haddie Charles. And she would be forever connected to Brad Caine by the baby conceived on the outskirts of a killing, a life beginning at the instant a life ended.

I had some doubts about some of the evidence Brad said existed, but I had no doubt he would turn over Kelly just like he said he would do. The choice became clear. Me or Kelly. One of us would go to prison or be executed, and one of us would not. I had to ignore feelings of revenge against Brad. What would happen to him could have no place in my decision. The bookend was the murder weapon just as he said it was. Fingerprints had been wiped away. The finger was the finger of Haddie Charles, gnarled and brown, with a painted fingernail. My fingerprints were on the briefcase, my letter of demand soaked in blood, and the D.A.'s office was convinced I filtered five thousand dollars worth of stolen cash through the trust account and called it a fee paid by Brad Caine. My past-due bills and debts filled a large cardboard box. Hell, I'm even left-handed.

My arrest, and later the guilty plea, was front page news. There was speculation and rumors about all the remaining jewelry, but I've never said a word one way or the other. I'm only able now to write this story because of what happened to Kelly afterward. Other than my lawyer, for the first two years in this place I didn't receive a single visitor. I didn't receive a single letter. One morning I was taken to the visitation area where I sat in a chair facing a sheet of plexiglass with an empty chair on the other side. I waited for several minutes thinking that maybe a mistake had been made. There would be no visitor, or perhaps a person would sit down in the chair, a stranger, expecting to see the face of their husband or son, and finding me instead. But then Becky appeared. She sat down and put the black phone to her ear.

I closed my eyes, not wanting to pick up the black phone on my side of the glass, not wanting to hear what she would say. It could only be bad. With my eyes still closed, I placed the phone to my ear and listened.

In a steady voice Becky said, "Kelly died last Saturday. We've already had the funeral."

I waited a moment and then opened my eyes to make sure she was still there.

"How did she die?" I asked.

"She overdosed in a hotel room in Biloxi. They found her alone. I've got custody of Jack."

I felt my eyes close again as I pictured Kelly in a dark cheap hotel room, alone, wrapped up in the sheets of a stranger's bed. A crazy place to finally find peace. When I opened my eyes again, Becky was gone. The black phone hung from its cord, moving slightly.

Brad Caine was right that morning when he said he would walk out a free man. Right in the legal sense, but how can a man like Brad Caine ever really be free? We have more in common than I care to know. Maybe I should have seen it coming. Maybe I could have stopped it all. But maybe, somewhere in the back of my mind, it was my only chance to try to repay a debt I could never satisfy. It doesn't matter now. The future is certain, and I will spend the rest of my days with this certainty. Brad Caine was right about another thing, there is indeed a difference between living and being alive.

Deborah,

Along with this letter you will find a handwritten manuscript of my story. I don't expect it to change anything, certainly not my legal situation, but I just wanted you to know the truth. The death of my daughter, Kelly, has allowed me to come to terms with what I have done. It allowed me to write it down.

I didn't kill Haddie Charles, but it doesn't matter. I am responsible for the death of Kelly in that hotel room in Biloxi as though I was there, brass bookend in hand, crushing her skull below the right temple with a swift and single blow.

In one moment, one barbarian moment, many years ago, I touched my daughter in a way God never intended. My intoxication, unhappy marriage, or disturbing childhood cannot mitigate the act. It cannot be explained or buried. It stands alone, without reconciliation, but I swear to God I never meant to hurt anyone. Intentions aside, I caused an explosion in my family sending each of us hurtling in different directions like shrapnel.

I've always respected you. It doesn't have anything to do with how you feel about me. The story is yours.

Jack Skinner

## ACKNOWLEDGMENTS

The existence of MacAdam/Cage is proof that God loves books. Without Pat Walsh, David Poindexter, Scott, Avril, Melanie, Cindy, Amy, Tasha, Anika, and the rest of those people, this novel probably would never have been written, much less published.

I have to thank Sonny Brewer for his guidance and friendship, and my secretary, Melissa Bass, the very best secretary in the whole wide world. But mostly I have to thank my wife, Allison, as well as Dusty, Mary Grace, and Lilly, for the freedom, love, and support necessary for this writer to write.